OVERSOUL
SEVEN
AND THE
MUSEUM
OF TIME

BOOKS BY JANE ROBERTS

OVERSOUL SEVEN AND THE MUSEUM OF TIME

by Jane Roberts

PRENTICE HALL PRESS

New York   London   Toronto   Sydney   Tokyo

Published in 1987 by Prentice Hall Press
A Division of Simon & Schuster, Inc.
Gulf + Western Building
One Gulf + Western Plaza
New York, NY 10023

Originally published by Prentice-Hall, Inc.

PRENTICE HALL PRESS is a trademark of Simon & Schuster, Inc.

Library of Congress Cataloging-in-Publication Data
Roberts, Jane (date)
    Oversoul Seven and the Museum of Time.
    Sequel to: The education of Oversoul Seven, and The
further education of Oversoul Seven.
    I. Title.
PS3568.O2387O9   1984   813'.54   83-19230

ISBN 0-13-647446-2

Manufactured in the United States of America

10 9 8 7 6 5 4

Dedicated to
Oversoul Seven
in All of His
Manifestations,
and to All of Those
Who Take the
Codicils
to Heart

Contents

Chapter One

Cyprus and Oversoul Seven
Look in on
Dr. George Brainbridge
and Friends

"I don't like doctors," Oversoul Seven said to
his teacher, Cyprus. The two of them were small specks
of light on the front second floor window of the small medical building.

"This doctor is one of your own personalities, and he needs your help," Cyprus said, sighing. "Souls aren't supposed to be prejudiced."

With that, the window flew open. A man in a medical white coat stuck his head out and started shouting at the pigeons on the small roof just below. "Beat it, beat it," he yelled; and the window slammed down.

"He needs help, all right!" Seven said morosely. "Is this an exam?"

"Exactly," Cyprus said. "And you're going to be his new associate.

1

You're going to adapt a physical body of your own for a change, and—"

"Never!" Oversoul Seven yelled.

"It's a necessary part of your education," Cyprus said gently. "You have to get closer to earth reality now to really understand your personalities' experiences. You knew it had to happen sometime." To comfort Seven, Cyprus turned into the image of a lovely young woman of ancient knowledge, or of an ancient woman with young appearance. Seven disconsolately turned into a fourteen-year-old boy. Both of them perched invisibly on the upstairs windowsill, above the Medical Center's circling paths. "This is really asking too much, Cyprus," Oversoul Seven said.

"Your personalities are physical all the time," Cyprus reminded him. She tried not to smile.

"How long do I have to have a   dy?" Seven asked.

"Why, just until you help Dr. Brainbridge with his problems."

"How long will *that* take?" Seven asked. His image blurred around the edges, and Cyprus answered, "Who knows? That's up to you."

"What *is* his problem?" Seven asked, uneasily.

"That's for you to discover too," Cyprus replied, looking nowhere in particular. "It will be readily apparent, though."

"I'd rather help Maha in the Land of the Speakers," Seven retorted. "Her life is exotic; or there's Tweety, growing up in the seventeenth century. Now, they need my help, too. It seems that I have more personalities than I know how to handle, and worse, you keep introducing me to more all the time. I didn't even know I had a doctor personality."

"You knew," Cyprus said, meaningfully, and Oversoul Seven blushed. "Well, all right. I knew and forgot; I mean, I thought he was doing all right."

"You gave him his life and energy," Cyprus answered, "and I know that you sustain him at one level, but you *do* need a follow-up."

"It makes sense," Seven said, in a dejected tone. Then hopefully, "Can't I just help him from here, though?"

Silence.

"I really have to take on a body for a while, not just an image?"

Silence.

"Digestion, breathing, all that?" he said, almost despairingly.

"All that," Cyprus said.

"Well, all right, for variety as long as I have to do it. I'll be a woman in the day and a man at night. Or I'll be an Indian on Thursdays, a Greek on Mondays—"

"*One* body," Cyprus said emphatically. "A man or a woman, take your choice. But you have to keep one body just like humans do, at least for this part of the examination. It has to be over twenty-one, too—say mid-twenties for this particular assignment."

Oversoul Seven was suddenly overwhelmed by the implications of the situation. "I'll have to . . . live someplace, then, I mean find a domicile or house, as it's called here; and wear clothes. Go into stores to buy them. I'll have to . . . relate to people; I mean, humans, as if I were one of them." He closed his eyes, so agitated that he changed into several images at once.

"Now stop that, Seven," Cyprus said quickly. "And do settle down. It's not all that bad."

"Not all that bad?" Seven was astounded now, growing more upset by the minute. "Helping my personalities out in the dream state, giving them inspiration, sustaining their lives is one thing! But . . . *joining* them is something else!" Now he looked like an old man, head bound with a turban; ancient and rickety.

"Pathetic image," Cyprus said, smiling.

"Do I have to be *born?*" Seven asked. "Nothing would surprise me now."

"No, there isn't time for that," she said. "You'll just appear."

"Well, that's something," Seven replied, a bit mollified. "I mean, birth implies such a commitment." Then as an afterthought, he asked, "What kind of a doctor *is* Brainbridge anyhow? A surgeon? General practitioner? A neurologist? A—"

"He's a dentist," Cyprus said.

"A dentist! I dislike dentists most of all," Seven cried. "They're butchers. In the twelfth century, a visit to the dentist is practically a death sentence, in just about every country of the world. The same applies to the seventeenth century, for that matter. Once my personality Josef almost died in a dentist's chair, though it was a filthy stall more than anything else, and—"

"Dr. Brainbridge lives in the late twentieth century," Cyprus said. "I checked medical histories in connection with time periods just to make sure you'd have the information you'll need. In this era, dentists are very, very respectable. And they are *not* considered butchers."

"They still *pull* teeth out," Oversoul Seven said, shivering slightly. "They don't use sound to dislodge them yet. Or to heal tissue, or—"

Cyprus couldn't help smiling. "See, you know a lot more about dentistry than you realized," she said. "Come now. Let's take a look at Dr. Brainbridge. . . . He's treating a patient inside. This is the Community Medical Building Psych Center, of Riverton, New York. George works there three mornings a week."

"Psych Center? What's that?" Seven asked.

"You'll find out. Watch—" Cyprus answered.

At first glance George hardly looked predisposing. He was stocky, brownhaired, with a flushed face and large lips and, Seven noticed, lots of white teeth.

"Haven't done any work on your teeth at all, have I? Well, today will take care of *that*," George Brainbridge said, and laughed. "Up in the chair, there."

"Verily," said the patient.

"*Verily?*" replied George, who was busily rearranging his tools of torture (thought Seven to Cyprus, who stood to one side, invisible).

The institution attendant, Mrs. Much, leaning against the door, said, "This one thinks he's Christ," and lifted her shoulders. She was dark haired, full in body, motherly.

George grinned at her and said, "Uh, oh. His appointment card says John Window, but that's O.K."

"Here we go," he said to the patient, who was now ensconced in the dental chair, his undistinguished face surrounded like a halo by the swivel lamp that glared almost in his eyes. "It's the molar," George said. "Just a little nitrous oxide here," he added, more to himself than to the patient. Then, "That's laughing gas. You won't feel a thing." He got out the round canister from his bag, saying, "You just squeeze this. You can regulate how much you need. If anything begins to hurt, squeeze. Got it?" He was peering into the patient's face; some could regulate their own doses and some couldn't. "I think you'll do O.K.," he said.

The patient's brown, curiously warm and deep eyes stared into George's. "I'm Christ," the patient said. "I can stand a little pain. Or perhaps I won't feel any at all. I'm never sure of my reactions. Gas won't be necessary, though."

The attendant moved slightly forward. Oversoul groaned mentally; but with only an instant's silence, George went right on talking as if he were used to having Christ in his dental chair all the time. "I'm not allowed to take out teeth without anesthetic," he said. "And

4

novocaine in a setup like this takes too long. So why not humor me and take the gas? It will make things a lot easier all around."

A pause. Then Christ shook his head. "Verily. Do as you want, then."

"Super, *super,*" George replied, rubbing his hands together. "Now, see how this works?" George demonstrated while the patient hesitantly took a few whiffs.

"Heavenly," Christ said. Oversoul Seven felt uneasy seeing the man in George's dental chair, his face brightly lit in George's lamp, his mouth now open as George peered inside.

"Take another sniff," George said. Christ complied. He smiled and began humming "Nearer My God To Thee" as the gas took effect, so that George had to tell him to open again. "Wider," George said.

Watching the procedure, Seven winced as George's pincers came down on a bicuspid in Christ's lower jaw. George applied pressure, pulled, and he had the tooth in his hand. "There, you did great. Super! There's the bugger," he said, showing Christ the tooth.

Christ was still under, smiling, and for a minute George Brainbridge stepped back in surprise. He'd never seen such a brilliant, uninvolved, innocent smile in his life. The patient was in his forties, yet right now his eyes looked like a boy's of ten. No, George thought: he had a kid of ten, and the kid never looked *that* innocent in his life.

"Bless you," Christ the patient said in a voice so peculiarly sweet and winning that George just stared, still with the tooth in his hand, bloody roots and all. And as the patient spoke, George Brainbridge felt his whole body suddenly, unaccountably become warm and tingly; it felt glowing, pliable, filled with strength as if he himself had become younger in the flash of an eye. Automatically he pushed a square of white gauze into the hole left by the tooth, and swabbed out the blood in the patient's mouth. All he could mutter, again automatically, was, "Super. You did super."

In the meantime, Oversoul Seven stared suspiciously at Christ.

"He always blesses everyone," said Mrs. Much, the attendant. She shook her head emphatically. "Never causes us any trouble."

George just nodded, trying to act as normal as possible. It was the gas, he decided, that gave the patient such a . . . a . . . sublime expression; he was euphoric, for God's sake, nothing mysterious about that. Except that George was feeling euphoric, too, and he hadn't taken anything; didn't even get a whiff. And how could you explain that? "You can get down now," he said, after checking the hole in

Christ's gum; it showed slightly and he said, "We'll fill in that hole somehow. Don't you worry."

Christ spat out a little more blood and hopped out of the chair as agile as a boy. He paused, turned to George and said, "Bless you again, my son," and made the sign of the cross. And this time George just stood transfixed. He literally felt as if his entire body had been tuned up, adjustments made here and there, circulation quickened and cleansed; as if he'd been breathing pure oxygen for years. Despite himself the words were out of his mouth: "How do you *do* that?" he sputtered.

"I'm Christ," the man said, gently enough, and though George reminded himself that this guy was some nut in the mental institution, the words made sense. Not sensible sense, George thought, but some kind of sense.

Mrs. Much chortled: "He gave you the whammy too, huh?" Her broad face looked amused but kind. "Suggestion," she said. "Amazing, isn't it?"

"I'll take a shot of that any time," George said. He made a long, drawn-out whistle and watched with unaccustomed awe as Christ waved goodbye and went out the door.

"Ciao," George said.

George took care of several more patients, but he didn't joke as he had earlier and he forgot to say "Super" to encourage his patients and reassure them. Everybody wanted to be a "good" patient, after all.

But George was upset about the Christ patient and he wasn't sure why. And *that* worried him. It was O.K. to be depressed because, say, a tooth hurt. So you had it pulled. Or your blood sugar was down. Or someone said or did something to anger you. Or somebody rubbed you the wrong way. Like this guy, George thought glumly. Because the patient, a young man named Gregory Diggs, was staring belligerently into his eyes.

"Open up further, please," George said, and he took a good look at the man's face just before he slid his gaze to his open mouth. "Feel this?" he asked, tapping, exploring the gum tissue, "You had a wisdom tooth out at the reformatory." He bent back up. "It's your gums, not your teeth, I'm afraid. Hurt quite a bit sometimes, don't they?"

"Yeah," drawled the young man angrily. He scowled resentfully. "How'd you know?"

"The gums tell all," said George, washing his hands. "They never lie. They're falling apart. They're—"

"Shit they are! You just want me for more appointments. You'll probably pull every tooth in my head just to make a few extra bucks!"

George had almost forgotten what was bothering him, but the young man's defiant, scornful glare brought it all back, because George instantly compared that hateful look with the forgiving, yet childlike clarity in the eyes of his earlier patient. The exuberance he'd felt when the nut first blessed him had vanished. Naturally, George thought, with irony. But his usual state of being—that had always been A-O.K.—now seemed drab and dull by contrast, as his whole body were full of novocaine.

"Well?" demanded the young man arrogantly.

"Hell, I pull teeth just for the fun of it," George said. "How come you're here?"

"The dumb bastards want to find out if I'm crazy or not."

"Are you?" George asked. "I think everybody is crazy. Can't say I'd suggest gum surgery. Don't think it would do any good."

The young man said, "You mean, if I had money, you'd do it, don't you?"

George had had it. He stepped back, hands planted on his hips.

"I'll take every tooth out of your head right now if you want me to," George said, with a forced laugh that was half joking menace and half real dismay. What the hell was wrong with guys like that? he wondered. Then, "The condition of your gums is so advanced that I don't think you can save the teeth anyhow. I'm trying to save you some pain. Gum surgery is no picnic, and I doubt it will help in your case. The teeth are loosening. In about three months or so we can start taking them out, and I'll give you a bridge for a while—"

"Shit, I'm not going to be here any damn three months," Gregory Diggs shouted. "You're a crazy man! In three months I'll be long gone one way or the other." He started to get out of the chair.

"Have it your way," George said, and he shrugged his shoulders because he couldn't get through to the kid at all. And, he told himself, he should have known better than to try.

"Yeah, well you done with me?" Gregory Diggs asked. "I got an appointment with my banker." He grinned, got out of the chair, wiggled his backside defiantly, and headed for the door.

"Super. Enjoy yourself," George said dourly.

George began cleaning up his equipment and packing up his instru-

7

ments in his small bag. Still watching, Oversoul Seven said: "Even though he's in an institution, that Gregory worries me. I don't mean to make too much of this, but—well, he couldn't hurt George in any way, could he?"

"Remember the existence of probabilities, that's all," Cyprus said. "I wanted you to have a good look at your personality's life and work before you're introduced into his environment."

"And the Christ character," Seven said. "People who think they're Christ worry me too. You never really know what they're up to. I still don't see why George was so upset when he felt better."

"You will," Cyprus replied. "Worry about that later if you must. Right now I want you to have a look at George's establishment. George is spending the afternoon and early evening at the cottage, with his wife." And as soon as Cyprus spoke, she and Seven were in George's downstairs offices, several blocks away. "Pay particular attention to the layout of the house," Cyprus said. "The family rooms are upstairs, for example. You're supposed to meet George for the first time for dinner at eight."

"Why should I pay particular attention to all that?" Seven asked. "I sense some implications . . . or complications. . . ." But Cyprus was gone.

Uneasily, Oversoul Seven looked around. Though everything looked normal, the rooms had an unsettled quality—a shifting or impermanent feel—as if they had only just taken their present form the moment before he arrived. Seven sighed. Despite his odd premonitions about the house, his first duty was to look it over, and then to meet Cyprus so they could settle the question of what kind of body he should take.

Seven whiled away the time by trying on various images for size, though he didn't thicken them into bodies—mostly because he didn't know how.

The time passed so quickly that it was evening before Seven realized it; and George, he thought, should be home at any time. He decided he'd better look the house over as Cyprus suggested. He went into the next room; just as he did, he took the immaterial form of a young man in his late twenties—the approximate age he'd appear in his physical body—when he got one. It was then he realized that something wasn't right: Everything was blurring, as if either time or space were being squeezed out of shape.

8

Chapter Two

The Right Place
but the Wrong Time.
The Right Name
but the Wrong Man.

Invisibly Seven swirled around, trying to get a
fix on the proper time and space and to acquaint himself
with the territory, so to speak. He knew that he had the space right,
for looking out of one of the windows through the lace curtains, he
saw the river a block away, the arching bridge, and the opposite
shore. The house lights were off . . . *lights?* Oversoul Seven gulped
and looked out the window again—those were gaslights in the street
instead of electrical ones. He was in the wrong time. In his preoccupa-
tion with his images, he'd let his hold on time slip.

Of course. Now he noticed the gaslight fixtures on the house walls.
He sighed, turned his inner attention to Dr. Brainbridge and his
proper 1985 time, and waited. But nothing happened. Moreover, something in the atmosphere of the house seemed strange in a way that

Seven sensed, but couldn't pinpoint. A consciousness was . . . wandering, perhaps slightly off course. He could almost feel a consciousness bumping up against concepts too big for it.

Oversoul Seven paused. His job was to get back to the right time, not to go wandering off by himself. But his curiosity was aroused, and his sense of adventure. Staying where he was, he let his mind travel throughout the house. Downstairs was a small dentist's office. To the left, bits of late sunlight glinted on the instruments. A smell of cloves and camphor . . . ugh . . . and chloroform. A waiting room was at the front of the house with two work shops and a kitchen of sorts to the rear.

Three bedrooms, a parlor, and kitchen took up the floor Seven was on. He was becoming impatient, until his mind suddenly caught a commotion on the floor above. He rushed upstairs. There in an attic room, on a cot, lay a man of about thirty. His consciousness was wandering berserk all over the place. Oversoul Seven saw the man's dream body, which had no stability at all, but was changing images constantly even while the man was hallucinating other images—so that the room seemed full of dragons and demons, with the poor fool, Seven thought, caught in one battle after another.

A demon with a wolf's jaws rose threateningly in front of the man's dream body. The man yelled out, started trembling and closed his dream eyes in terror, just as Oversoul Seven turned into the image of an old wise man, told the demon to disappear, and led the frightened dreamer back toward the cot.

It was then that Seven noticed the paraphernalia—hidden partially behind a chair—and saw how the dreamer had come to such a predicament. "You've been sniffing gas," Seven said.

The two of them sat side by side on the cot. The man was still in his dream body. "I do it all the time, up here alone, while my wife and son are away for the summer," he said. "I'm experimenting. But who are you? I must still be under."

"You're under, all right," Oversoul Seven said. "By the way, what year is it, and who are *you?*"

"Why, I'm George Brainbridge. Dr. Brainbridge," the man said, in a surprised voice, as if he thought that his name was a household word. And as he spoke he leaned toward Seven rather formally, and held out his hand.

Oversoul Seven was dumbfounded. "Dr. *George* Brainbridge? You're sure?"

"Well, my good man, I certainly hope I know my name," Dr. Brainbridge said. "And who, pray tell, are you? I'm not exactly sure what's happening, but this is by far the most delightful encounter that I've had under these circumstances—"

"Uh, what year did you say it was?" Seven asked. He was almost afraid to hear the answer.

"It's May 21, 1890," George said. "You mean, you mean, you don't know that either?" His voice grew excited, and *looking* at him, Oversoul Seven got his first real *look* at George Brainbridge the First. He had sandy hair, frazzled right now, a sandy beard, and light blue eyes that were shaped like the electric Christmas tree lights that he, George, would probably never live to see; and he had two dimples on his left cheek. As George's eyes lit up with excitement and expectancy, Oversoul Seven immediately knew George for what he was— a dreamer, an idealist, forever caught between dreaming and acting.

Oversoul Seven just groaned: "You're the wrong George Brainbridge. I'm in the wrong time period; but if my calculations are right, you're far too old to be George's father. It must be your grandson I want."

The gas hadn't begun to wear off yet. George Brainbridge now thought the entire affair was magnificent. "Well, while you're here, let's talk," he said agreeably. "I keep a journal of my gaseous activities, as I call them, and what an entry this will make." He rubbed his chin, reached for a pipe, and prepared to settle himself for a long chat.

Without thinking about it, Seven hallucinated a pipe for George, who didn't realize that he was still in his dream body; then Seven said moodily, "I've got to think my way out of this because your grandson—he *must* be your grandson—needs me, and I don't even know what trouble he's in."

"Ah," said George, dreamily.

"Ah?" said Seven, a bit loudly. "A lot of help you are; sniffing gas and hallucinating demons and God knows what. . . ."

"I heard William James talk about nitrous oxide and determined to try it myself," Brainbridge said, huffily. "I consider my activities as explorations, pure and simple, into the nature of . . . of truth."

"That sounds pretty pompous to me," Oversoul Seven said. He didn't mean to be unkind, but he was worried about returning to the proper time period, and at the same time he was growing more and more aware of his surroundings and the nineteenth-century sum-

11

mer twilight. Indeed, the scents rushing through the opened window grew clearer and more tantalizing. He wiggled his nose and breathed deeply.

"Those are lilacs you smell," George Brainbridge said. "They're planted on one side of the drive. French lilacs and white ones. You can still smell the appleblossoms, too. They're planted by the barn—"

And suddenly Oversoul Seven was so enchanted by the odors and by the late sunlight on the white lace curtains, and by the sky showing beyond that he just stared at George in amazement. "In the midst of this beauty, this sensual bath of light and scents, why would you bother looking for other realities . . . ? If you really felt . . . what this moment demands . . . you'd be so filled with life that you'd sense what truth was, and you wouldn't need to go looking for it."

"That was a beautiful sermon," George murmured drowsily. Just before he closed his dream eyes, he muttered, "Grandson? I don't have a grandson. . . ." His dream body fell back into his physical one, and George Brainbridge was finished with everything but sleep.

Seven sighed. He eyed the sleeping George with a mixture of exasperation and relief, and covered him up with a crisp white sheet that had been folded neatly by the bed. But why, he wondered, had he become so mixed up in time? Did the gas-sniffing activities of the nineteenth-century George have any bearing on the problems of the twentieth-century grandson? The house, Seven mused, was the same. So the space coordinates were the same for both men, though obviously they focused in different time periods. But why, why, had the wrong George attracted him?

Because *something* had attracted him, Seven thought, or he would have gone undeviatingly to the right George. Seven sighed again; here he was, all alone in some nineteenth-century attic, in the right house, but some hundred years away from where he should be. Worse, usually such errors were somehow self-corrective, or else Cyprus bailed him out. But this time the environment was remaining stubbornly stable. He couldn't seem to move one minute ahead in time, much less a hundred years—or eighty-five: what was the difference?

Seven stared dejectedly at the floor where Dr. Brainbridge's paraphernalia still lay. He had to get back to the twentieth century, where he *would* form a body and live in it for a while. A short while, he hoped. In the meantime, he noticed that the sky was beginning to darken. He looked out the back window of the attic, down through the twilight mist at the wooden barn, smartly painted a dark red. A horse neighed from inside; and then he heard a very clear distinct clippa-cloppa sound, leaned out, and saw an iceman in his horse and wagon. The man wore a green cap with white stripes on it, and a bright green jacket. He stopped the wagon, went around back, picked out a big block of ice and sprinted to the backporch, just beneath the window buttress where Seven couldn't see him; he reappeared, and leapt back into the wagon.

Seven smelled warm manure mixed with the smell of the lilacs, and in the next moment the mist lifted so that the purple flowers stood out all dewy by the driveway below. A delightful scene, Seven thought; and he *liked* the gas-sniffing George Brainbridge a lot better at first sight than he did the twentieth-century version who chased the pigeons. And as if he'd called them, a flock of pigeons came swooping down from the back side of the barn to the buttress beneath the window; and began cooing. From the cot inside the room, George Brainbridge muttered, "Goddamned pigeons," and Seven despite himself began to laugh. Then he sobered. He had to get back somewhere close to twilight, 1985. And quickly.

Chapter Three

Oversoul Seven
Takes a Body
and Finally Meets
the Right George

Cyprus was a speck of light in the office waiting
room of George Brainbridge's twentieth-century residence.
George was waiting in the office across the hall for the arrival of
his new associate, Dr. Seven. George whistled under his breath, turned
on the radio, squinted at the pigeons on the window ledge, and hoped
to hell that the new arrangement was going to work out.

But Cyprus could tell that Seven was either waylaid or had taken
a wrong turn in time or space; he wasn't in *this* space in this time.
Slightly exasperated, she loosened her own consciousness from its
precise orientation with time, but maintained the same space coordinates. From her present probable position her consciousness went
whirling through the room's futures. Still no Seven! So Cyprus started
to ruffle quickly through the past.

Almost at once she saw Seven wandering around, a good hundred years off—but in space hardly a few feet away. She materialized as the ancient-but-young woman teacher and stood beside him. George Brainbridge, glancing into the waiting room in *his* time, saw no one, of course.

"Seven, you're in the wrong time," Cyprus announced.

"I went back into the past," Seven cried, "and met George's grandfather." He was wearing his favorite fourteen-year-old male image.

Cyprus smiled; almost. "I didn't realize that you were methodical enough to do such background reference," she said.

Seven smiled modestly.

"I thought maybe you just got lost," Cyprus said.

Seven blushed. "Well, there must have been a reason why I ended up in the wrong time with the wrong George," he said defensively.

"Exactly," Cyprus replied. "Remember that later. But you don't even have a real body yet, and George expects you at any moment."

"You *do* mean a body, not just an image?" Seven asked.

"A *body*. I told you that before," Cyprus replied, laughing. "And you have to make it in the right time period, so it will fit properly. That means that we have to return to the twentieth century first."

Seven looked dejected. "How come you're so much better at time travelling than I am?" he asked plaintively. "Sometimes I have no problems, and then . . . well, I get confused."

"All right," Cyprus said. "Look at that chair beside you." Seven did as he was told, studying the red velvet Victorian armchair until it suddenly shimmered and became the leather rocker in George's twentieth-century waiting room. "That's the easiest way for you to do it now," Cyprus said. "There *are* better ways, and before long, you'll know what they are."

"Where *is* that guy?" George muttered from his office.

"Well? Where's your body?" Cyprus demanded. "Isn't it ready?"

Seven sighed. "I haven't even had time to think about a body, much less do anything about getting one," he said disconsolately.

"We just can't have your body suddenly appearing from nowhere in the middle of the room, either," said Cyprus. "Stop pouting, Seven. Come over here, around the corner, where George can't see you from his office."

They stood by a corner of the fireplace in the waiting room. "Now," Cyprus directed. "First, adopt the image you want. A young man is best; about twenty-six years old will do. As for the rest, use your imagination."

15

Rather regretfully, Seven dismissed his fourteen-year-old image entirely and started over. He stood six foot three. His hair was almost black, and bushy. He added a beard, then removed it. First his eyes were blue, then he changed them to brown. "What about the mouth?" he asked Cyprus.

"Hurry, Seven," she said scoldingly. "Decide on one clear image and let that be that."

So Seven changed his hair to a bushy dark brown, added a rather high forehead, a resolute jaw (so he'd look trustworthy). The mouth just seemed to come of itself; it belonged to the fourteen-year-old image he liked so well, except that its mischievous humor was modified by a slight turn downward. "That's it," Seven cried.

"All right, now," Cyprus said. "Try to keep your consciousness as clear and still as you can. This will just take a moment."

Seven wasn't sure exactly what Cyprus did then, but he felt his image slowly solidify. Invisible atoms rushed from the four corners of the earth to congregate within the form. He felt tremendous activity. Then, in a flash, he felt the activity from *inside*. A heart was pumping blood; the blood flowed through the brand-new veins. His pulse started like a tiny clock. Seven grinned, trying out his facial muscles. He'd been inside a few of his personality's bodies before, to help them out for one reason or another, but this was different. A body of his own! A strange sense of possessiveness overtook him. This living parcel of earth belonged to him; let no one trespass!

"I see the experience isn't so undesirable after all," Cyprus said drily. "But there seems to be something you've forgotten."

"What?" Seven asked. He looked down at the elastic flesh, and felt within it the ambitious inner organs . . . all snapping to attention. "Everything's there, as far as I can see."

"Seven," Cyprus said, meaningfully.

Seven grinned brilliantly. "Oh, the clothes. I forgot the clothes," he said.

"Precisely." Cyprus shook her head. "I hope you've done your homework and know what garments you want," she said. "Now make an image of the clothes, and I'll fill them in."

Seven was actually quite proud of himself. He formed the image of undershorts figured with appletrees, and a black turtleneck undershirt. Cyprus quickly turned these from images into real items of clothing.

"How do you do that?" Seven asked.

"The same as with your body," Cyprus replied. "I haven't time to explain. I cause the . . . atoms in space to thicken . . . and congregate. But what else do you need?"

"The *pièce de résistance,*" Seven answered proudly, and on top of the underclothes he formed the image of a dark green polyester suit, with the tiniest of green and white checks. "What do you think of that?" he asked. "Perfect late 1980's."

"Well, you *do* look like a young dental associate," Cyprus said, doubtfully.

"I hope so," Seven retorted. "I studied and studied and studied so that I'd be sure to fit in."

"It's just that I didn't realize that dentists in this century went barefoot," Cyprus said, laughing and staring into Seven's new bright and astonished brown eyes.

Instantly Seven formed the images of socks and black boots. "The socks are treated with deodorant," he said. "I saw some like them in George's dresser. Most of these clothes are based on his wardrobe . . . so he *has* to like the way I dress. . . ." When Cyprus continued to laugh, he said defensively, "Well, there's an awful lot to remember. Your humor's at my expense. . . ."

"You just look so . . . so *earthy,*" Cyprus replied, trying to control herself. "You have no idea; you look like a young dandy."

"I don't," Seven protested. "I look like a young dental associate. You said so yourself."

But suddenly Cyprus was serious. She filled in his socks and boots. "Remember, your body is only a temporary one," she warned. "And treat it kindly. There are some things you're used to doing that you can't do with it; and some places it won't go. But you'll learn all of that."

"What places?" Seven asked, a bit alarmed.

But Cyprus had no time to answer. Again George Brainbridge muttered loudly, "Damn, where is that guy?" This time he came out into the hallway. Cyprus said, "Quick, walk to the hall so it looks as if you came from the waiting room." And she vanished.

Dr. George Brainbridge (the Third) was thirty-nine, slightly stouter than he should be for his unimposing five feet, 6½ ". In fact, Seven thought he was a trifle jowly, and his brown hair was nondescript. His moustache and eyebrows were both rather shaggy, but extremely expressive; both were moving, it seemed, all the while. And George Brainbridge's eyes, though small and a bit sunken, were—well, dynamic. People probably didn't notice George's eyes much, Seven mused, because he kept them half closed a good deal of the time.

17

But then, whammo; they opened wide, all the way, usually to express an amazed appraisal of the person to whom he'd been talking so mildly. And sometimes the eyes grinned all by themselves.

Right now, George's eyes did their grinning act as he looked at the newly-minted Seven. "Super," George said. "You must be my new assistant."

Young Dr. Seven smiled and stepped forward, extending his hand in the accepted Earth fashion.

"Super. Super, super," George Brainbridge said again, squeezing Seven's new hand so tightly and with such force that Seven almost felt like whimpering. "Tonight's garbage time, though. I have to stack the garbage cans outside. It'll only take a minute. And drive to the corner store for some pickles. Whole trip will only take two minutes. Then you and I can relax, have a few drinks and eat dinner. Make yourself at home. Be right back."

And before Seven could even answer, George bounded toward the rear of the house, leaving Seven flabbergasted—and a bit annoyed: All that rushing on his part just so George could pile the garbage!

And here he was alone in the house again. A house that just wasn't trustworthy, he thought. Then almost without thinking about it, he went into George's twentieth-century waiting room.

"I never should have called the house untrustworthy," he said later to Cyprus. "But of course I did. And it was."

*C*hapter Four

Up and Down
the Time Staircase

Of course, Seven realized that the house had changed through the years since George-the-First's time. For one thing, there were two water marks indicated by small gold plaques showing how far up the walls the water had risen in the floods of 1948 and 1972. The two plaques were set about two feet apart, one above the other, just to the right of the marble fireplace in the waiting room. In the first George's time, this had been a parlor and the fireplace had been workable. Now it just sat, elegant but useless; a decoration. Above it was an innocuous still life of flowers. Oversoul Seven grimaced at it and looked out of the narrow floor-to-ceiling front windows. Set right before them were huge pots of plants that instantly took Seven's attention. He was only vaguely aware of the cars speeding by just past the front sidewalk, in a certain

19

rhythm, as the traffic light at the corner by the bridge let swarms of traffic by. Then there was a pause until the light turned green again.

The house was built of the sturdiest red brick, so that even on this warm June day it was cool inside; and possibly the bricks muffled the traffic sounds, even though a window was open. In any case it was during one of the pauses in traffic that Oversoul Seven suddenly realized that something was wrong—again! There was a thick maroon rug on the dark wooden floor, but none in the entry way behind him. And Seven realized that he'd been hearing footsteps cross the tiled entry floor from the front door to the stairs. They'd been pacing, he realized, for some time, though no one but himself should have been in the house.

Seven whirled around, astonished, for he caught sight of George Brainbridge the *First*, just going up the stairs. Simultaneously, the sounds from the window seemed terribly different than they had only a moment ago. Seven spun around again. He stared, quite incredulous.

Both the nineteenth- and twentieth-century streets existed at once; or nearly. The automobiles were clearer than the horses and buggies, but only by a hair. The houses across the street shimmered back and forth from their nineteenth- to twentieth-century appearances, and back again. A new house kept disappearing and a lot took its place. The lot changed to the house again, so quickly that Seven blinked.

He turned back toward the room to rub his eyes, but to his dismay, the process hadn't been confined to the outdoors. Objects from the nineteenth-century drawing room kept appearing in the waiting room—or rather, the waiting room kept turning into the drawing room. One mohair chair suddenly appeared, bumping Seven in the knee. He leapt back. A huge fern sprang up in the far corner.

The coffee table beside Seven vanished and was replaced by a Victorian tea table, complete with a pot of tea, three cups and a bouquet of early summer roses from the yard. Actually, Seven saw, it was as if everything pulsated, but so quickly that he couldn't keep track. Everything shimmered and vanished, but not before a second group of objects already began to appear.

He stared and squinted. There was no time where there was nothing, but always at least the indication of an appearing or disappearing object. So when the roses appeared again, Seven grabbed the vase and held it to see what would happen.

20

"It wasn't a very bright move," he said later to Cyprus, who agreed. Because the vase and flowers trembled, shook, shimmered—and so did everything else in the entire room. Then, as if the room had made up its mind, the vase and roses settled down to be themselves. The Victorian tea table stayed. The flood watermarks were gone. The room didn't change back again, and Seven found himself standing in the wrong place and the wrong time.

Seven gulped. Surely, he thought, this must be happening only to his own perception. That is, the twentieth-century house would be there for George the Third when he came home from stacking the garbage and buying the pickles. Wouldn't it? But there was no time to consider George the Third because Seven suddenly heard someone come in the back door—and anyone who came in *that* door would find him, physical body and all, where he didn't belong. In his consternation, Seven dropped the vase. It crashed into pieces on the floor.

In a flash, Oversoul Seven rushed to the stairs, running on tiptoe as quickly and quietly as possible, heading for George the First's private attic study. Seven's heart was pounding. He was sweating. He thought that at any moment someone would come out of a bedroom to see him racing down the dark hall of the second story. It surprised him that a body could move so fast, but he was panting by the time he reached the door to the attic steps. He opened it, overcome by relief, and stood resting against it on the other side.

It was then that he heard George the First laughing.

Seven was all ready to go through the door to George's study when he remembered that he had a real body, even if it *was* in the wrong time. He lifted his hand to knock at the door, then just stood there, pondering: George probably wouldn't let him in; and worse—he wouldn't recognize him because when they'd met before, Seven was in a wise-old-man image.

"Oh. Ah. Haaaa, haaa. . . ." The sounds from the closed door drove Seven to distraction. He had to talk to George and find out what the connection was between his sniffing gas and the time changes. "And then, the solution came," he told Cyprus again later. "I saw the closet, and from then on I knew what to do." Seven went quickly into a small closet to the left of George's door, sat his body nicely down, hidden and out of the way. And then, pleased with his resourcefulness, he just left his body, took an astral image of a wise old man, and walked through George's door.

George Brainbridge the First giggled slightly and said, "So you've

21

come back! Here, have a sniff. I've made the most astounding discovery."

"How come you always see my astral form when you're sniffing gas?" Seven demanded. "And what have you been up to? I just saw you downstairs a few minutes ago and—"

"Hush, hush, hush, now," George said. Then in a happy singsong voice he went on: "I saw . . . I saw . . . the future. I saw this house in the future. . . . I even saw a book on dentistry that's in the library where it can't be, of course. But it is."

"Well it won't be there for you now," Seven replied glumly. "We're back in your time now. What did you do to . . . make it happen? I'm supposed to be in the other time, the future one."

"Zounds. A problem," George said, in the same singsong voice. "That is, I haven't the faintest inkling of how or why it all happened."

Really worried now, Seven sat down on the cot beside George. The late afternoon sunlight filtered through the lace curtains and glinted here and there on the rose petal pattern of the wallpaper. The carriage house door had been left open and the carriage was gone. The maple trees were full of singing birds. The white doily on George's old bureau moved gently at the edge by the window as the soft breeze blew in. George lifted the small canister, took another sniff of gas, and said dreamily, "I hardly ever get to come up here during the day, but several patients cancelled their appointments . . . ah, how lovely . . . a day in June it is." His moustache quivered, his brown eyes smiled fondly at Seven, and he snapped his suspender straps gently back and forth. "Whoever you are, welcome again and again," he murmured.

And Seven thought: The carriage was gone from the carriage house, just as George the Third's car was gone from the garage. Did that mean that George was still at the store?

"I'm going to write down the name of the book I saw, too," the George beside him said. "It will prove that I *was* in the future somehow. Maybe I'll even inform that personage, William James, about my story. . . ."

"You can't prove anything," Seven said, crossly. "The book won't be discovered in your time by others—" As soon as he said this, Seven figuratively bit his tongue, because George's eyes suddenly glistened. "You're right," he said, "I'll have to steal it somehow; and bring it back with me. If the time change happens again, that's what I'll do."

"No, no, no, you mustn't do that," Seven cried. "I grabbed ahold

22

of a vase of flowers in your parlor when the times were changing back and forth, and when I held the vase, I got the time that went along with it."

"My mind is clear as space," George said, wonderingly. "You're saying that if I steal the future book, I might wind up there."

"Exactly," Seven said, reminding himself of Cyprus.

George half-closed his eyes, leaned backward, and negligently played with the tassels on the belt of his maroon dressing gown. He wiggled his shoeless black stockinged feet and said smugly, "That would be most auspicious."

"Auspicious! It would be disastrous," Seven cried. Just as he spoke, a sound from below caught his attention.

"Zounds, it's the carriage," said George. "The housekeeper, Mrs. Norway, must be returning from her visit with her aunt. I suppose I'll have to make myself presentable and—"

"Will you be quiet!" Oversoul Seven cried. He was thinking as fast as he could. If the carriage was returning in *this* time, then just possibly the car was pulling into the driveway in 1985—with the right George Brainbridge in it. Seven ran to the window.

The carriage came slowly past the peony bushes. Seven waited until the horses drew up to the carriage house—apparently Mrs. Norway was taking them all the way inside the barn, ignoring the hitching post. Then with all his might, Seven imagined George's small Porsche car. He saw every detail in his mind and he kept trying mentally to transpose the desired shape of the car over the carriage. One of the horses neighed, distracting him, and behind him George the First muttered dreamily, "What are you doing now?"

The carriage shimmered, the horses disappeared, the car came into position, and then the horses and carriage (and Mrs. Norway) returned. Seven gasped because the Porsche *also* remained. Mrs. Norway got out of the carriage, apparently without seeing the automobile. George Brainbridge leapt out of his car, slammed the door, started whistling, and ambled up the sidewalk. And then, both he and Mrs. Norway went in the back door.

Seven didn't know what to do. Beside him, George the First stood up, straightened out his dressing gown and shoved the gas canister under the cot. When he turned around Seven was gone. George shook his head, said, "Zounds" beneath his breath, and thought that there was no telling how long the effects of sniffing lasted.

Seven was afraid to go out into the hall; he hoped against hope that when he left George's study, somehow he'd be back in the twentieth-century house. No such luck, he thought, finding the hall as it had been before. He stepped into the small closet where his body was sleeping comfortably. He dove into his body as quickly as he could, even though several questions instantly came to mind.

Who would see his body, for example? If Mrs. Norway saw him, in the nineteenth-century house—well, he was in trouble. He reeked of the twentieth century, decked out as he was in a summer polyester suit whose style and material would be quite strange to her. To say nothing of the digital watch—a nice touch, he thought, though that at least he could hide in his pocket. He couldn't change into either of the Georges' clothes, because both Georges were too short and pudgy for the body Seven had decided upon. While he was thinking about all this, Oversoul Seven very gingerly walked down the stairs to the second floor, which was *still* nineteenth-century. And then, with his heart in his throat he started down the front stairs that came out in the front entry.

Or suppose George the Third saw him, Seven wondered; then that would mean that George would experience the house in the *past* as Seven was. Didn't it? Or—he shuddered—suppose both George the Third and Mrs. Norway saw him simultaneously. Or suppose. . . .

He stepped onto the slate floor of the entryway. At the same time, both Mrs. Norway and George the Third approached, though the room itself was solid nineteenth-century. "Back," George announced. "Chores all done. Super!" he said, bounding across the room. He loosened his tie, tossed his light summer jacket over what appeared to be a nineteenth-century armchair, and said, "I've got some great new jokes, though."

"Ah, zounds," Seven said.

"*What?*" George asked, surprised.

"Uh, I mean, super," Seven replied, blushing and realizing his mistake. "Uh, do you see anything different about the house? Or that chair?"

Seven felt dizzy. As he spoke to George, who obviously saw him, Mrs. Norway (who obviously saw neither Seven nor George) was bending over the broken vase on the rug and murmuring, "Now how did *that* happen?" Seven closed his eyes a moment in true despair.

"What's wrong with the chair? It looks O.K. to me," George said. "Everything looks O.K. to me. It's been a super day, garbage or no garbage." He grinned at Seven, sat down (in the mohair chair, as far as Seven was concerned), and said, "Well, what have *you* been up to?"

Seven shook his head, and suddenly began laughing. Tears fell down his face. George Brainbridge the Third was so pragmatic, so focused in his time and place that, well, anything else would seem an impossibility. And as Seven laughed, a part of his consciousness merged momentarily with George's, and through George's eyes Seven saw the twentieth-century room just as it had always been as far as George was concerned. And in that instant, George the Third unknowingly endeared himself to Seven forever after.

"What's so funny?" George asked, beginning to laugh too. "Is there egg on my face or something? Did you sniff some laughing gas from my canister?"

Seven laughed louder; here was the down-to-earth George in the present, perceiving his usual environment, come hell or high water, while upstairs and ninety-five years away, his grandfather couldn't even begin to keep his times straight.

"I don't know," Seven gasped. "You made me laugh, something you said or didn't say. . . . As George's face broke into a new cheerful grin, Mrs. Norway vanished, the tea table disappeared, and Seven was back in George's twentieth century, where he belonged.

Chapter Five

A Would-Be Thief
in the Night

They sat at the kitchen table. "We have this
whole second floor as our living quarters," George said.
"Usually it's noisy as hell, but with Jean and the three boys at the
cottage, it sure gets quiet."

Seven grinned, imagining George surrounded by young sons.

"Shit," George said. "Last weekend I started enlarging two rooms
at the cottage, but you could *still* put the whole place in the middle
of *this* house and have room left over! No one builds houses like
this one any more."

Thank Heaven, Oversoul Seven thought, enjoying his own joke.
But the dinner was excellent. George half considered himself a gour-
met cook. In fact he wore an old apron over the summer shorts he'd
put on after work. Seven stared at George's thick thighs with some

begrudging admiration, and wondered if he should have made his own thighs larger.

"My parents and their parents must have had thousands of suppers in this same spot," George said, musingly.

Seven almost said, "I wish you hadn't said that," because as soon as George mentioned his grandparents, Seven imagined them sitting at the 1890 summer table.

"I'll say," George answered. "It's spooky in a way to think of it. And these old houses. They're being torn down through the city all the time. This one has really been kept up, though. So has the neighborhood. But it *is* decaying. The town would love to make it into an urban renewal project."

Seven nodded but he wiggled uncomfortably. A sense of menace suddenly assailed him. He looked around. The back dining room was brightly lit. Beyond it, out the second story windows, the yard was disappearing in twilight. Then someone said, "Here's the smart-assed dude's place," and Seven looked up in surprise. "What?" he asked.

George raised his bushy brows. "Nobody said anything."

"Uh. I must be hearing things," Seven replied, and he smiled brilliantly.

In his confusion it took Seven a minute to realize what had happened. He'd forgotten that humans heard only spoken conversation, though he tried to keep it in mind; and according to the rules, he had paid attention only to words. But in the instant that he forgot, he'd picked up someone's thoughts—and they didn't belong to George. . . .

"Uh, I thought I heard something downstairs," Seven said finally.

"Naw. It's just the house; it makes noises all the time," George replied, helping himself to some dessert.

"What would anyone want to steal down there?" Seven asked, insistent.

"A few drugs in my office, is all. Now and then some joker breaks into a dentist's or doctor's office." Unconcerned, George said, "Come on. There's no one down there. Besides the car's out there. So anybody could tell that we were home. . . ."

But Seven was now following the menacing thoughts from room to room downstairs, from the back to the front of the house. He finally located them in George's office.

And for once, Oversoul Seven didn't have the slightest inkling of what to do. The thoughts he "heard" told him that the man downstairs was full of hate and rage; but also full of indecision, scared to death. If he told George about the intruder, Seven thought anxiously, he'd have to play by physical rules. The police would be called, the thief caught; for he *was* a thief . . . even now he was picking the lock of George's drug cabinet. Seven started coughing to hide his confusion, and to give himself time to think.

"Oh, I'll get you some water," said George. Seven coughed harder. George stood up and slapped him on the back. Seven, suddenly realizing what a body felt like when it was slapped, stopped coughing. "Uh. I'm all right," he said, blushing.

"Look," George said. "Let me do up the dishes. You go down and relax. Got a bedroom for the night all ready. Then we'll have a couple of beers."

"*Super,*" Seven exclaimed, getting up so quickly that George looked startled. But Seven was still aware of the intruder.

Rather pleased with himself for dispatching George so cleverly, Seven started very quietly and somewhat cockily down the stairs toward the first floor. Surely he could take care of the culprit in some ingenious fashion. Then suddenly Seven stood still with dismay and foreboding. For one thing, a suspicious shifting was taking place in the air; innocuous paintings lined the staircase and they were . . . dissolving at the edges or trying to; and the old nineteenth-century oils were peeking through. While Seven was thinking, "What an awful time for time to start shifting again," he remembered something vital that he'd forgotten in his desire to protect George's mortal frame. He, Seven, had a physical body now, too, which meant that dealing with the unknown culprit wouldn't be as easy as he'd hoped.

That thought came to mind just as Seven came to the entryway and saw a young man hastily going through George's desk in the office. The door was open; and the thief worked with a flashlight that he turned off as soon as he heard Seven's now-hesitant footsteps.

Again, the house's contents seemed to shimmer. The young man crouched down and Seven saw him clearly in the glare of the streetlight—before it turned into a dimmer gaslight; and Seven made an inaudible moan. He was about to advance in any case when he heard new footsteps pounding down the stairway behind him. "Zounds. Who's here?" thundered George the First, descending the stairs with a hunting rifle.

As quickly as he could, Seven turned on the light switch, and the gaslights lit up the room. In the office, Gregory Diggs stared, mouth open, too astounded to move or speak. The room looked like a movie set, and the man who stood at the bottom of the stairs was completely unbelievable. He wore a dressing robe with tasseled belt, pince-nez glasses that looked a hundred years old—and he had a rifle.

"Oh wow, this is screwy," said Gregory, shaking his head from side to side. "I don't want no trouble. . . ."

"You blackguard," George shouted, advancing. "What's in that bag?" He rushed over, yanked Gregory aside, and pulled out the bottles and vials that stuffed the bag to the brim.

Dazed, Oversoul Seven watched; how could George the First see the thief in the twentieth century? How could the thief see George? And why didn't *either* of them see *him?*

"Sit right down, there," George Brainbridge demanded, pointing to the dentist's chair.

Gregory was shaking. "I came to the wrong place, I guess. I was trying to get even with a guy."

"Even with a guy, huh. What kind of talk is that?" George thundered.

"I didn't know *anybody* had gaslights no more," Gregory murmured, staring at them. "And that outfit; man, where are you at?" He was feeling a bit more confident now, because George had put the gun aside, though it was still within his easy reach.

"Don't either of you see or hear me at all?" Seven asked, looking into George's face.

"You got everything back," Gregory stammered. "I was just gonna sell the stuff."

"Open your mouth," George demanded.

"What?"

"Open your mouth," George said. "Your breath smells: There's something wrong in there. A man's house is his castle, you young whippersnapper. Don't you know that? Open wider!"

"You gonna torture me?" Gregory cried. "You're some kind of pervert. Oh, Jesus." He was near tears.

Oversoul Seven gave up. He sat down in the corner as George shouted, "Hell, no. I'm a man of good will when I'm not crossed. Look at that! What kind of meals do you eat anyhow? Your gums are a mess."

"My gums?" Gregory gasped. It was hard to talk with George's fingers in his mouth, and Gregory still wasn't sure the guy wasn't going to pull his teeth out by the roots or something.

"Come from a poor family, do you?" George demanded.

"Uh."

"Nobody's all bad. That's my policy," George said, warming up to the subject.

"This is no time for a sermon!" Oversoul Seven yelled, but George didn't hear him.

Catching on, Gregory Diggs said sadly, "Very poor family. We don't have nothing." But he was feeling more sure of himself now that he had a handle on George. A bleeding heart liberal was a push-over.

Testing, Oversoul Seven tried to pick up a pair of scissors from a small table. His hands went through them. But the thief had a body—and he was from the *twentieth* century. Seven had to figure out how George and the thief could see each other at all.

"This will make you feel better," said George, taking a bottle from a drawer. He took the top off and the smell of cloves almost took Seven's breath away.

"Hey!" Gregory cried but George smeared some all over his gums, the competent fingers pressing in, so that Gregory shrank back in the chair. He was thoroughly scared again. Here he was in a dentist's chair like one he'd never seen before—with a gaslight shining in his face—and the pressure from some nutty dentist's fingers driving his gums mad. Besides he felt saliva gathering all over his mouth and his eyes stung. "Tender, huh!" George said.

Seven was getting panicky. He didn't seem to be able to affect *either* environment, and his own body felt strange and disconnected.

Chapter Six

A Challenge
of Probabilities

Seven kept trying to speak, but again no one
heard or saw him. Worse, an odd shifting seemed to take
hold of everything—not just the furniture as before, but the very
house itself. It was as if space speeded up through time . . . or as if
time speeded up through space; Seven couldn't decide which. But
the walls themselves began to flutter almost like wooden curtains,
and then to break up into beads, and then into dots.

Seven realized that the walls had vanished. He stood alone, on a
grassy knoll, in a warm dark night. The house and Dr. Brainbridge
and the thief—indeed, the entire neighborhood—were gone. Yet
Seven was sure he was in the same place, though he wasn't sure
just how he knew this. A soft wind blew past his face, and then he

saw that the river (the same river?) was still approximately the same distance away.

Seven was more upset than he wanted to admit, because his experiences thus far had seemed to lack any kind of organization—or rather, while he could perceive some order, he didn't seem to know how it worked at all. Before, the house had given *some* orientation. Now it was gone. Besides this, Cyprus seemed to have abandoned him, at least for the present; *any* present, he thought, dejected.

He looked about. As far as he could see, the area was entirely wooded except for the small clearing on which he stood. Where or when was he? "Cyprus?" he called, mentally. But there was no answer.

Was this the spot on which the Brainbridge house stood? If so, from the viewpoint of the house's existence, was he in the future or the past? Seven looked up. Three globes glittered in the far distance above the earth. He groaned and tried to recall earth history. The first floating city was in operation in the twenty-third century; he remembered because one of his personalities—Proteus—lived there. The second floating city came around the twenty-fifth century and the third wasn't habitable until . . . until the late twenty-eighth century. Oversoul Seven let himself drop down on the uneven but grassy ground as he recognized his unhappy predicament. By his reckoning, it was about 2985 give or take a couple of centuries; so even if he was in the right space, he was a thousand years off his target!

Worse, Seven didn't dare walk outside of the area where the house was—or had been—because that must be the focus of whatever was happening. If he just sat there and thought back to the twentieth-century house, perhaps time would reverse itself. But the environment itself was rather unsettling. There were no ground lights at all, and from his position, the floating cities were no brighter than stars. A very fine rain was falling, so fine that it was more like a mist, and the grass was wet, and the trees made a murmuring sound as the water fell from one leaf to another. Otherwise, silence.

Why a thousand years in the future, where before he'd only bounced back and forth between the nineteenth and twentieth centuries? "Cyprus," he called, and again there was no reply.

Seven shivered. His body was wet, and though the air was warm enough, the rain had soaked through his polyester suit. No wonder mortals carried umbrellas, he thought, miserably. Nor did he dare leave his body while it dried out, for fear a time reversal might come and whisk his body off without *him*. But how was it that all of this happened when he still had a body on?

Cyprus existed in every time, and so did he, Seven mused, so he couldn't be lost. But he *felt* very lost indeed. If he remembered his history properly, in one probability, the earth in this century was a largely uninhabited planetary reservation area designed to protect nature, with visitors restricted. In another probability, though, the planet was nearly dead, bearing the lethal debris of countless nuclear wars. And in still another probability, it was just in the process of developing a new civilization.

But Seven had no way of knowing *which* future he was in, except that it "grew out of" the Brainbridges' presents—both of them!

Despite himself, Oversoul Seven noticed that the area was bathed in a soft mysterious air that now seemed enhanced by the rainy mist. In some strange way, the landscape seemed enchanted *and* enchanting. On the other hand, it also possessed a quiet waiting quality—as if it were a stage, in the few moments before a play was to begin. . . . Or, Seven thought suddenly, as if he were witnessing a probability-in-the-making.

And was this the Brainbridges' earth?

Before Seven could even begin to answer his own question, the sky exploded with images, and he saw a picture of such multidimensional proportions that he didn't know where to look first—much less how to interpret what he was seeing. The vision was so vast and astounding that he felt his consciousness struggling to expand its reach to contain it. The entire scene was one world with areas laid out in various time periods. The architectures and agricultures and technologies were changing in each segment and the people were all wearing the unique clothes of their times—and yet (Seven saw) they moved from time to time as mortals now moved from place to place.

There were dazzling cities and the most primitive huts, all in glowing mosaics; there were factories and stone tools—and the emblems and flags of countries and religions and causes of which he'd never known.

Then—abruptly—a particular person's figure would take prominence in a particular mosaic. The person (sometimes a male, sometimes a female) would make a simple motion—lift a vase, raise an arm, turn away. And as if in response, all of the other segments would change, too. Different kinds of buildings would appear, or an army or a vast parade would rush into action. But as these persons executed their simple motions, the entire panorama was completely altered in one way or another.

33

As Oversoul Seven tried to interpret his experience, he almost lost himself in his concentration. In one mosaic, for example, a woman in 13,000 B.C. picked up a simple tool—and in another mosaic, a spaceship took off. *Then*, however, the order of motion was reversed. The astronaut pushed a simple button on an instrument panel—and as if in response, the woman picked up her tool.

Then, so quickly that Seven couldn't follow, he saw George Brainbridge the First in his private attic study; a miniature, but glowing with intensity. And the Victorian George was peering out of the attic window at the very scene Seven was witnessing. At the same time, George the Third appeared, also in miniature, the antiseptic white dentist's office like a tiny brilliant white closet against the sky; and George was looking down into the face of Gregory Diggs, the thief. The two of them were seemingly frozen in the same position forever, even while Seven had the feeling that the relationships between them were constantly changing. And again simultaneously, in another mosaic the patient at the mental institution who thought he was Christ suddenly held up his hand, as if to stop the entire cosmic production. And at once everything vanished—except for the landscape, which was again filled with mist.

The wind had an unusual murmuring sound as if voices were hidden in it somewhere—a hypnotizing, compelling, yet distant sound. Seven listened, knowing that whatever he was "hearing" wasn't sound as he was used to thinking of it; but an inner molecular rustling as if the atoms of the rocks and trees and grass were all trying to speak, or manufacture tongues, at once. The "sounds" changed several times until Seven finally made out their message: *The Codicils*. But what did that mean? The inner sounds were more like vibrations that he translated into words, so that the very ground beneath Seven's feet vibrated; and so did the misty trees; until from everywhere those inner words, *The Codicils*, came rushing into Seven's mind.

"What are *they?*" Seven asked mentally. But the moment he asked, the vibrations ceased. And Cyprus stood beside him.

Cyprus looked more radiant than he'd ever seen her. Besides this, she seemed to have a kaleidoscope of images at her command, so that as she appeared, other images of herself cascaded from the main one; images of men and women of all ages and countries and times sparked out onto the landscape and then exploded like firecrackers. Seven was almost abashed at Cyprus' abilities. He felt quite powerless in the midst of such a display, as he stood there in his polyester permanent-press suit, now more than slightly damp in the night mists that had returned.

In fact, by the time Cyprus settled upon one image—the ancient woman with young appearance, or the young woman with ancient knowledge—Seven felt quite dejected.

"I certainly am glad to see you," he said. "But I haven't the slightest idea of what's been happening. Even with a body, I can't seem to stay in the right time. And you saw the world vision I just saw?"

"I saw it," Cyprus said gently. "You perceived more of it than I thought you would. Part of it you'll interpret as you go along."

"But none of my experiences seem *orderly* lately," Seven cried. "There's order there, I know! But I keep losing it. . . ."

"You don't lose it," Cyprus said softly. "It's there. You put off perceiving it, for reasons you'll remember later. But I have some important clues to help you.

"There's an important dilemma, or rather, an important period of change approaching . . . Now on the one hand, this change has happened, of course, and on the other hand, from the standpoint of George Brainbridge in the twentieth century, it hasn't. He's approaching a vital intersection of probabilities, and *you* must learn to help your personalities in the probable areas of their lives as well as with the problems they're aware of. . . ."

But Seven was truly dismayed. "You don't mean I have to handle a group of probable Georges?" he cried.

Cyprus smiled and ignored the outburst. "Remember your vision," she urged, in a tone he'd learned to pay attention to. "Important clues are there, too. Remember the personalities you saw in it, Diggs in particular. And remember, even for mortals, not all experience is physically manifest. Each person, Seven, is partially responsible for the birth of probable worlds . . . There, don't frown. You're doing very well. Your suit is most appropriate too—exquisite twentieth century; quite quaint."

"You're just saying that to cheer me up," Seven protested. But before he could finish, Cyprus said, "Get back to your main-line century for now though, or you'll end up more confused than ever. And don't forget, there's a reason why George the First perceived Diggs."

"I'm more confused than ever," Seven complained under his breath. "And how come my body travels through all those probabilities?"

"You'd better get that young thief out of the house before the twentieth-century George catches on," Cyprus said. "Worry about the rest later."

Cyprus vanished, and so did the thirtieth-century night landscape. Seven stood (fully visible, he realized) in front of George Brainbridge and the twentieth-century thief. The house still had its Victorian appearance. "Who in thunder are you?" yelled George Brainbridge the First, seeing him this time.

This time Seven concentrated with all his might. "Out, out," he shouted at Gregory Diggs, and he shoved Gregory out of the twentieth-century door. This time, he really felt his own muscles move.

Almost at the same time he turned to George the First and commanded him to rush back up the nineteenth-century stairs. Eyes ablaze with astonishment, George did as he was told.

Chapter Seven

The Transformation
of Gregory Diggs

Gregory Diggs crossed the street outside of
George Brainbridge's house, walked the half block to the
river by cutting through back yards, and sat down on the grassy
riverbank to think. A few cars passed above him to the right, sweeping
over the bridge, but the night was quiet. The air was still warm
though damp, with a mist rising from the water. Way to the left
was the soft glimmer of downtown lights. Gregory smoked a cigarette
and debated.

He'd planned to steal the dentist's drugs and sell them for some
ready cash; and *that* hadn't panned out. Not that it was his fault.
Even a genius couldn't have anticipated the nut who'd discovered
him—and thinking of it, Gregory started laughing so hard that he
rolled on the ground. A house with gas lights, yet, and a clown who

dressed like a dude from another century. Oh, God! He gasped. Now that it was all over, the comedy struck him. The guy who sent the other one upstairs must have been his keeper or something, Gregory decided.

But he stopped laughing—even if he didn't get the drugs after all, he was damned lucky he got off so easily. Only he *did* need some cash, and if it wasn't for his goddamned gums hurting him all the time, he'd just take off. The social worker had told him that the clinic would fix him up, but all the stupid dentist said was, "Too bad." A lot of good that did, Gregory thought, getting angry as he remembered; he'd still rip the bastard off if he knew where the hell he lived. Both men must have the same name. At least the nutty dentist put cloves on his gums, which helped some.

Gregory started walking, rather dejectedly, toward downtown, on his way to the health complex beyond. He had no other place to go, he mused; so what the hell? He wasn't even sure of his status there; he wasn't an outpatient but he wasn't an . . . inmate either. He'd sneak back in, he decided, and after breakfast, maybe take off for good. So he was out on bail. Caught stealing from a supermarket. What was that? All the judge said was that he had to stay under observation for a few days . . . Observation?

He grinned. Nobody paid any attention to him. He wasn't in any security area, though they had one. And in the day the place was mobbed with outpatients. All he had to do was just walk out again, if he wanted to.

He passed the backs of the downtown buildings, looking up at the rickety fire escapes that rose from the riverbank, thinking that those places would be easy to rip off—but would hardly be worth the bother. Nobody who lived there had anything worth stealing.

Two more blocks, and the grounds of the mental health complex were visible: low buildings, some with outside patios, trees in front planted in geometric patterns, a playground, a huge hospital-like structure with decorated bars at the upper windows. It all looked like some ideal neat modern village, Gregory thought, suddenly catching his breath because the whole place was bathed in the soft light from downtown that diffused through the clouds.

"Dirty bastards," Gregory muttered not knowing exactly who he was thinking of, but the peaceful uncluttered area with its trees and shaded small pathways sure as hell seemed to offer something that wasn't being delivered.

In his mind's eye, Gregory already saw himself walking across the back expanse of lawn, right up to the building he'd left so secretly, and right through the bottom window to the small room and cot they'd given him. Maybe they hoped that he *would* run off, to another town—one less problem for the town officials.

"Shit," Gregory said. Despite himself, the softness of the June night was reviving his spirits. He sat down on one of the red benches by a small bed of flowers, and smelled the moist air that rose from the river. It was a crappy life, he thought, even as he felt his spirits rise. Still, the night was so comforting that he decided to stay where he was. If anyone questioned him, he'd say he couldn't sleep and came out for a walk. Now he was drowsily aware of his gums again, but suddenly he was too tired to care and he fell asleep on the bench.

When he awakened, it was sometime just after dawn. Not only did his gums hurt now, but two gumboils had apparently developed during his sleep, and the tip of his tongue was sore. Gregory grinned, and tried to ignore his difficulties, though, as he remembered the events of the night before. Best of all, he hadn't stolen anything, even if he *had* intended to, so nobody new was after him. And he was on the honors system at the clinic division of the mental-health place. He grinned again, ambled over to the main building, climbed in his window, and sat down on the bed.

There were early noises from the security section of the building where the mentally disturbed were kept; and from somewhere, the smell of coffee. Gregory got up, went down the corridor whose walls featured glossy snapshots of the city and valley, and came out finally in a large room. The new sunlight poured through five east windows, leaving five brilliant paths upon the linoleum floor. In one corner, a television set was turned on, though no one was watching it. There were various kinds of chairs about the room, some upholstered in floral patterns, a few bean chairs, several tables, and lamps.

At first Gregory thought he was alone, but then a noise at the further end of the room caught his attention. The sun was so bright that he could hardly see, but in the glare he made out a man's thin figure. "Uh, hi," Gregory said. "Any idea where I could get some coffee or aspirin around here?"

The figure came closer. The man, in his forties, wore dungarees, shirt, sneakers, and carried a broom. "Custodian," he said.

"They start you working early, huh?" Gregory asked.

"Verily," the man answered.

"Verily? That's a funny thing to say," Gregory replied. "Cigarette?"

"Don't mind if I do," the man said, setting the broom aside.

Gregory grinned: he'd been lonely, he thought; and this guy seemed engaging in a way he liked at once. He lit the man's cigarette. "Keep the joint clean, do you?" he asked.

They sat down facing each other, a small table beside them. "I'm Gregory Diggs," said Gregory, amazed at his own politeness.

"My real name is John Window, but I think I'm Christ," the man said, smiling. "You might as well know right off."

"Aw, you're putting me on?" Gregory said, blushing despite himself. "I mean He's dead, for one thing. And you don't look dead to me."

"That's a fact," the man answered.

"You don't look like you're nearly two thousand years old, either," Gregory said, with a jerky laugh. But he was fascinated. "Hey, I heard about you a few days ago," he said. "Why do you think you're Christ? What do the psychologists say? How come they let you around like this? I mean, you could just walk out of this place."

"Where would I go to?" the man, Christ asked. "I have an advantage on myself. I know Christ's history. They'll crucify me if I leave here, and the doctors know I won't go any place. Besides, I have jobs to do here."

Gregory's eyes had never been wider. "Yeah, like what?" he asked. The sun hit his eyes again, and he had to turn his head.

"Oh, I go about my father's business," the man answered. There was a sly hint to his voice, or so Gregory thought, so he turned back to look closer at the man's face.

The sunlight hit it almost directly as the man also turned; and for a moment the custodian's face looked hazy, unformed, glimmering. Gregory sprang up without a word and snapped down each shade to the bottom of each window, then went back to his chair. "Couldn't see," he muttered.

"Blessed are the blind, for they shall see God," the man said sweetly.

"Now, see here, that's enough of that," cried Gregory, feeling a trifle uneasy by now. "Do you know where I can get aspirin? My gums are killing me. They got some disease, the dentist here says."

"He took out a tooth of mine," the custodian said sympathetically, and Gregory started laughing, no longer frightened. "Well, that proves you aren't Christ," he said. "Christ could fix his own teeth, couldn't he? So you can go out in the world now and not worry about being crucified." Suddenly, though, Gregory's tone changed. "They won't hang you to any damned cross anyhow. But they'll get anybody they can. You don't have to be Christ, you know, to be crucified in this world."

"That's a fact too, I guess," the custodian answered, and for a moment Gregory felt that he and this odd stranger were united in some way, or at least understood the world in the same terms, or *something*. The momentary rapport between them made him uneasy too, so he said in a brusquer voice, "My gums . . . I guess my damned teeth are going to fall out."

And Gregory was never sure exactly what happened next, or who spoke first, he or the custodian. He only knew that once again, the sun nearly blinded him. Colors of all kinds kaleidoscoped through his inner vision; yet at the same time, there was a whiter-than-white pattern as well. . . . Through all of this, he glimpsed—or thought he glimpsed—the custodian's face, close up, with the most compassionate smile imaginable.

The custodian spoke, and Gregory felt the words, but couldn't understand them with his ears. In the next moment a tingling warmth spread through his face, gums, jaws, and eyes. The warmth was somehow almost dizzying, and he felt—he *felt* his teeth tighten in his head.

There was the warmest pressure as each root dug itself in deeper; and tiny hot snaps as the gums tightened around them. Gregory was caught up in so many emotions that he could hardly identify them. His tongue slid across his gums—no gumboils! And the tip of his tongue didn't hurt. He opened his eyes. Then he saw that the light wasn't nearly as bright as it had seemed only a moment before, because he had, after all, pulled the shades. Then where *had* that light come from? "The . . . the . . . light," he muttered.

"Not as bright as it was a minute ago. The sun just dimmed some," said the custodian, looking more or less, Gregory thought, like any man in his forties; no halo, for Christ's sake, no . . . *power* such as he'd just sensed.

"Feel better? Gums okay, huh?" the custodian asked. And when Gregory heard his voice this time, there was no doubt in his mind that somehow or other this man had completely healed his gums. "How . . . did you do that?" he stuttered. "I don't know what to say. Nobody ever does anything decent for me, much less. . . ."

"Now and then I *can* work miracles," the custodian said. "I don't mean to brag, though, it's just my way. Now I have to finish my chores. Don't tell anyone, though. Miracles always cause trouble for me." He picked up his broom and began vigorously sweeping the floor.

"But . . . but you shouldn't be here doing *that*," Gregory shouted. "You healed my gums! You could make a million dollars. You could . . . My God, how did you do that? I feel fantastic all over. . . ."

"Do what?" the custodian asked, blinking now as if the sun suddenly hurt his eyes. "Aspirin and coffee can be got two doors down."

"Hell, who needs aspirin?" Gregory shouted happily. "I never felt better in my life. You healed me, or something." Again he said, "But how did you do that?" He couldn't hide the awe in his voice.

"Shush. I'm just the custodian now," John Window said, almost in a drawl. There was a sly closed look about his face; and yet a secret smile belied his proclaimed ignorance. He moved rather loosely toward the television set and stood watching the program in progress.

"You thought you were Christ a minute ago," Gregory yelled, scandalized. "You just . . . did the impossible. How can you pretend nothing happened?" In his bafflement, Gregory grabbed Window's arm and half swung him about.

There was no doubt that Window was suddenly frightened. "Don't tell anyone," he said, in a new, low, quavering voice. "When I think I'm Christ, sometimes I do things that can't be done. But I know who I am now. I'm John Window, and that's a fact."

The sunlight now had a hard yellow cast, an objectionable glare. Gregory backed away from Window scowling. It was a game Window was playing, he realized—and not a nice one. Window was terrified of . . . well, whatever . . . power he had. So Gregory said, "That's all right. I'll play it any way you want. Don't you worry, everything will be okay. Cool it. Don't get upset."

John Window's eyes fluttered just slightly. It seemed to Gregory that one powerful ray of strength or understanding—or compassion—travelled from Window's eyes to his before the custodian turned his back and ambled away. No, Gregory thought, watching. Window was shuffling, where before his steps had been quick and sure.

Gregory couldn't believe what had happened, and he couldn't *not* believe it either. What was Window so frightened of? he wondered, because he recognized real fear when he saw it; he felt it himself a good deal of the time. Window wasn't feigning *that*. But what was he so scared of, and why should someone with such . . . *power* fear anything?

He watched until Window disappeared into another room off the main corridor and then, forgetting he'd wanted coffee, Gregory

42

drifted out to the lawn. The mental changes in himself weren't at first obvious, though the physical ones *were;* and he tested these at once. Grinning, he tugged at his teeth, *tugged,* and they were as firm in their sockets as teeth could be.

He still couldn't get over it. The soreness had been with him for several years, too; and without it he felt almost giddy and light. But more, he felt like running, really running—not away from anyone as usual, but just for the joy of it. So he stood up and ran as fast as he could across the street, behind the buildings, to the riverbank. It seemed that in some way he couldn't fathom, the trees and sky and riverbank were all his—his and everyone else's, too. He ran up and down so buoyantly that he was laughing out loud until finally he felt drained—and ready to think. He hardly remembered crossing the street again and sitting down on the same bench on the psych center lawn.

By now it was nearing 8 o'clock. Outpatients and center attendants began arriving for the day, parking their cars in the lot to the left. Gregory stared at the people; they looked okay on the outside, he thought, but they wouldn't be there if they didn't have troubles. And inside, unknown to the doctors or psychologists or *dentists,* was some guy they all thought was a nut. Only that nut could do things that could make people right.

Gregory tested his teeth again; what would he do if they suddenly wobbled? But they wouldn't, he thought triumphantly, remembering and still feeling the unique sense of certainty that he'd experienced when . . . when the custodian did whatever it was he did. There it was, Gregory realized, the thought he'd been putting to the back of his mind: He wasn't exactly sure if the man had actually touched him, or only looked at him. But what difference did that make? This Christ had credentials!

He breathed deeply, freely, noticing something else. Until up to right now, he'd always breathed tightly. It felt as if he had more room in his lungs, or as if his lungs had more room in his ribs, or. . . . And that thought clued Gregory in to a further realization: his fear was gone. Here he was, sitting on a bench like anyone else, not wondering what people thought of him, or if he looked like a bum, or if some cop was going to challenge him just because he always looked as if he'd slept in his clothes for a week, which he usually had. He even found himself smiling at a passersby; not faking it, either.

This almost awed him as much as the tight teeth. When he thought *that*, a delayed reaction set in to a change of mind that had been going on ever since he left the custodian. Now Gregory *was* dizzy with elation: for the first time in his life, he thought, someone had done something great for him . . . and without wanting anything back . . . and without his asking. He'd always taken it for granted that the worst would most likely happen unless you did something to prevent it, and his twenty-one years of experience seemed to prove his point—up to now. He felt half embarrassed, but there was no doubt of it; the universe or God or chance or just the fates had unquestioningly somehow blessed his presence. And not just with a trifling pat on the back, but by giving him suddenly proof of. . . . His thoughts boggled. Proof of what? He didn't believe the guy was Christ, for instance . . . but when *Window* believed he was Christ—wow!

And the guy responsible, Gregory thought, was locked up inside the psych center, frightened, probably afraid that the authorities would find out about his abilities, and do what? What *could* they do? he wondered. Kick him out on his ass, Gregory supposed. Then he remembered: When he believed he was Christ, the custodian also was sure he'd be crucified.

Well, he wouldn't be—not in any way, shape, or manner, Gregory told himself resolutely. And in that moment, Gregory felt the first strong purpose of his life; he was going to help the custodian somehow, someway. It didn't occur to him that he was thinking of someone else for the first time in his life, too. The big question in his mind was, *How* could he help?

"I'll just walk right into the newspaper office and tell my story," he thought, imagining an awed reception, the reporters interviewing Window, Window healing the masses of people who came to see him. . . . But then Gregory's smile faded; *that* would scare the custodian to death. "Shit," he muttered. It was then that he felt almost inspired—or at least the solution came instantly to mind. Before anything else, he had to show the dentist the change in his mouth. Oh, Christ! Tears of laughter fell from his eyes as Gregory imagined Dr. Brainbridge when he saw those tight teeth in the healed gums. What could he say? What could the poor bastard say?

Chapter Eight

Dr. Brainbridge Is Confronted
with Proof of the Impossible:
or Is He?

Gregory Diggs found out that Dr. Brainbridge
worked at the psych center only two mornings a week,
so it was two days later that Gregory stood waiting in front of the
dentist's office in the center's main building. He was nervous, he
realized, no doubt about it. He suffered from a bad conscience, knowing that this was the man he'd intended to rob only a few days earlier.
He still didn't know if he'd been in the right place or not, or if the
odd character in old-fashioned clothes was a demented relative of
this dentist's or what. Gregory fidgeted: and who was the younger
man who had finally let him go? For all of Gregory's desire to tell
his story and prove John Window's abilities, he hadn't dared go back
to Brainbridge's house. So now he waited impatiently as Dr. Brain-

bridge walked down the corridor, with Seven stepping smartly beside him.

Seven and Gregory recognized each other at once. Gregory started to bolt, certain that the story of the attempted robbery must be out—but in a flash, Seven grinned, put out his hand and said, "A patient who can't wait to get in, huh?"

Confused, Gregory managed a smile half guilty and half filled with gratitude.

Dr. George Brainbridge said, "You aren't on my appointment list today, are you?"

Brainbridge opened the door at the same time, and Gregory pushed in past Seven. "I have to talk to you. Just a minute. You've got to see something."

He was almost pleading, and his manner toward George was so deferential that George grinned quizzically and said, with a half laugh: "Not out to get me today?"

"I'm done with all of that. Look at this," Gregory cried, opening his mouth as wide as he could.

George shrugged, adjusted his glasses, started to say, "What happened? Lose a tooth?" when, looking, he gasped, cried "Jesus Christ, sit down there," and shoved Gregory over to the dental chair.

"Open wider," he demanded. Gregory did. George let out a long whistle and said to Seven: "Look in this kid's mouth, will you? Tell me what you see."

Wonderingly, Seven looked. "All fine and dandy," he said. "Uh, super."

And George Brainbridge, his face flushed, said, "That's what I was afraid you'd say."

"Surprised, I bet?" Gregory said. He laughed as George put his hand into his mouth and started tugging at the tight teeth.

"Jesus," George said. "A few days ago these teeth were damn near ready to fall out; so bad in fact I figured the kindest thing to do for Greg here was to let them do just that." He shook his head, and looked at Gregory. "What happened?" he asked. "I've never in my entire career seen anything like this. Once started, the tissue just gets more diseased, and in the condition you were in, the thing was way past any reversing. It just doesn't happen."

"So you told me," Gregory said with relish.

Oversoul Seven let his consciousness dip toward George's and found himself astounded at George's inner reaction. It was as if Gregory's healed gums had set off a series of psychological quakes in George's

46

mind. He believed what he saw in Gregory's mouth and yet he couldn't; he kept looking for ways of dismissing the evidence obviously before him. His stubborn denial completely baffled Seven.

And Gregory, after laughing out loud triumphantly, now found himself feeling sorry for the dentist.

"*What* happened?" George demanded again. He was red-faced.

"You probably won't believe me," Gregory began.

"After this, I'll believe anything," George muttered.

Now when it actually came time to tell his story, Gregory found himself embarrassed. Only his determination to help the custodian kept him from running from the room. "I don't really know," he started. "My gums hurt like hell. I got two new gum boils from when I saw you. Then yesterday morning, I met this custodian in the entertainment room. He was sweeping up and we talked. . . ." Gregory gulped, and looked directly into George's eyes. His voice went high and scared and wavery. "This guy looked at me or did something, and suddenly I felt my teeth tighten in my head. I mean I *felt* them tighten. I got hot all over and saw lights. . . ." He broke off, his telling of the story finally making him aware of its impact; of its impossibility—and of its definite truth. Briefly he lifted his head and cried, "It's that guy I told you about, the one who thinks he's Christ. He did it, I mean, he really did."

Oversoul Seven tried to look impressed, but he kept his mouth shut so he wouldn't say the wrong thing. A body and a polyester suit didn't necessarily make you human, he thought, rather confused. And it certainly didn't make some human views any easier to understand. He wanted to shout, "Miracles, as you call them, happen all the time. That's nature unimpeded," but he said nothing of the sort. Instead he tried to understand why George and Gregory Diggs both seemed so shocked, and why Gregory was almost near tears.

George Brainbridge rubbed the corner of his nose, blew his nose, adjusted his glasses for the tenth time in ten minutes, sat down, and threw out his nearly-pudgy arms in astounded dismay. "Well, if it happened, it happened! I mean, no dentist could have fixed those gums in ten years, much less two days. There's no way you could have tricked me." He said this last to Gregory, but with a desperate question in his voice as if wishing that he *was* being tricked. Indeed he said, "I'd almost rather it *was* a trick than face—well, what those healed gums imply. . . ." He took the cellophane off a fresh patient's glass, filled it with water, and drank it down quickly.

Gregory just watched him. He was trying to recover his own com-

47

posure. Then he said, almost apologetically, "That's not really all. But my whole body's felt terrific since. I mean, fantastic. And well, I'm not so, you know, paranoid about people." He looked embarrassed.

With a sudden rush of despairing humor George said, "Well, every silver lining has a cloud."

Gregory managed a wan grin and glanced toward Seven. "I've done some things I'm not so proud of," he said, with a slight question in his own voice.

Now that he'd told his story, he began worrying that Seven might tell Brainbridge about the attempted robbery. . . . But Seven gave Gregory a brilliant grin and said, "Put all that behind you."

Seven had been so quiet that George almost forgot he was there. Rather startled, brought back from his own thoughts, he said emphatically, "Right, right." Then, after a pause, he shook his head again with new perplexity. "Had to be suggestion. It's the only answer. I mean, that guy John Window is a nut. At least he certainly isn't Christ. But suggestion—shit—how can suggestion heal gums in a minute that were in the shape yours were in? It can't."

With more courage than he knew he had, Gregory said, "That guy may not be Christ, but he's okay. I mean, he *knows* that he thinks he's Christ sometimes. And he's harmless. But not only *that*, man, think of how many people he could cure. Maybe he could even cure cancer!"

"Whoa, whoa. Super!—a whisk of the hand and you're cured—" George planked his hands on his hips. "I can't quite see that," he said, almost vehemently. Then, with true exasperation, "Open your mouth again, will you? And Seven, get me this kid's dental records from the file there. I want to see that diagnosis in black and white. . . ."

Seven got out the records. George flipped through them, holding up Gregory's with the tip of his fingers as if it were made of fire; he eyed it gingerly, unbelievingly. He shook his head again and said, "Well, there you are. Dated four days ago. Advanced periodontal disease."

Looking at the record, his worst fears confirmed—that something impossible *had* happened—George determined to face the impossible with determination, vigor, and a sense of humor. His pragmatism made him face the fact of . . . a most unusual event! That's what it amounted to, he decided, just as Gregory asked, in a worried tone, "What are you going to do?"

"Do?" George repeated. "Hell, what's to do? It's done. I might like a little talk with that custodian though. Or then again, maybe not. Give me a bit of time to think about it. I'd like to see those gums of yours tomorrow, anyhow. . . ."

"You won't get Window in any trouble, will you?" Gregory asked, sounding more worried than before. "I mean, well, his abilities challenge the authorities, don't they?"

"They sure as hell do," George answered. He was caught, because though he was nominally a member of the establishment, his sympathies were usually with the underdog—which was one of the reasons he helped out at the center to begin with. But . . . his conventional knowledge of medicine and dentistry made him scandalized at the apparent healing—it flew in the face of all common sense knowledge. Moreover, he was beginning to remember his own encounter with the Christ patient. This made him more nervous than before. "Look, I've got three patients lined up for this morning," he said. "I'll think about this and I'll get in touch with you. We'll put this thing in some kind of perspective. . . ." Gregory didn't want to budge, but Seven gave him a friendly shove, and led him to the door.

"I'll be in touch. I promise," George assured him. After Gregory left, George did two extractions and a filling without saying another word to Seven except for, "Just hand me that thing-a-majig," pointing to an instrument for which Seven had learned the proper name but *not* George's pet designation. So Seven was kept hopping, anticipating what George would want next, and following the gesture of George's arm as his fingers pointed generally to the area in which the instrument could be found.

"Now, the digger," he said, and when Seven promptly handed him the tool, he murmured, "Super," but in a distracted, automatic way. Even his reminders to the patients to open wider were made without his usual accompanying smile.

When the last patient left, George looked at Seven and shook his head. "I am truly mystified. For the first time in my life, I just do not know how to react. What's your opinion on all of this. . . ?"

This time Seven forgot himself in his desire to help, so he said, "What's the problem? The boy's gums were definitely healed. Miracles are nature, unimpeded."

George's eyes snapped open. "That's an odd thing to say. Miracles are nature unimpeded, huh? Bullshit! Something's going on beside just the healing of gums. Come on now, do you think we've been hypnotized?"

"Hypnotized?" Seven asked, astounded. Where could George ever get an idea like that?

"Or maybe we're hallucinating?" George went on lamely. "Nope. Well, I don't know about you, but I'm hooked. I've got to find out what happened. Some kind of gimmick's got to be involved."

As they talked, George and Seven locked the office and left the building and headed for the parking lot. The June afternoon was warm, the day a soft green-grey. Every time he visited the center, George passed the playground, but this afternoon, talking with Seven, he paused and sat down on a swing. Seven sat on the swing beside him. There were no children around this time of the day, and only a few patients strolled the grounds. The sounds of traffic from the nearby main street were partially muted by all the shrubbery, and Seven and George sat, not speaking for a moment.

Then George said, "You're an odd one. You know? You're taking all this damn calmly."

"What is, is," Seven said lightly.

"Maybe it's because you're younger. I don't know, but at least when I went to dental school, they taught us that some things were absolutely irreversible; certain conditions. Hell, I'm chairman of the cancer drive."

"The drive for cancer?" Seven said incredulously, "Who wants that?"

"It's no time for jokes," George replied. "If *one* cure like that can happen, it shafts the entire medical profession. Instead of drives for dollars for technological advances, we'd have to . . . hell, *I* don't know, reexamine our ideas about the entire body, or find healers, for Christ's sake, or. . . ."

"Well, you know where *one* healer is," Seven said innocently.

"Yeah, in a nut house, where I'd say he belonged—if I hadn't seen that kid's gums for myself." Suddenly George sat bolt upright. "I've got it," he shouted. "There are two kids. Yes, that's it! They're twins, one with good gums and one with lousy ones. It's a goddamned con game!

"Twins," he gasped, laughing so heartily that he was half bent over, sitting in the swing.

Seven just stared.

"Oh, Christ! How could I have fallen for that?" George shouted, between laughs. "That little bugger's out to get me just because I couldn't fix his damn gums. I mean, he thinks we're all shitheads, members of the establishment, and that we couldn't care less; we get paid anyhow."

As hard as he tried, Oversoul Seven couldn't understand George's reaction. Why would George prefer that fraud was involved in the first place? And why was George growing more jovial by the minute? Finally Seven said, "You don't think there was any miracle at all, then?"

"Hell no, you're too gullible and well-meaning," George said, still laughing, but more softly. He swung back and forth gently, studying the toe of his right shoe as if the answers were contained within it. "Look," he said. "That Christ chap had to be in on this, too. Twin One shows me his lousy gums, then Twin Two shows me his healthy ones and says that that "Christ" healed him. But where do they expect to go with it from here? Miracles! Boy, was I ever taken in."

"I don't suppose you believe in the soul either, huh?" Seven asked, a trifle plaintively.

George stood up to stretch his legs. "I believe in teeth and gums," he said, grinning. "And they don't lie."

Within the context of the relationship between himself and George, Seven could only say so much; and he didn't even know how to say that, he thought miserably. But he looked at George with just the slightest touch of severity and replied, "There's more to life than teeth and gums, though."

And at once he saw that he'd hurt George's feelings, because George sat back down on the swing, slapped Seven lightly but disapprovingly on the shoulder and said, "Yeah? Well, listen. Being a dentist may not be the most heroic profession in the world—as you'll find out yourself before too long. But I'll tell you one thing: People are damn grateful when a bad tooth is extracted, or you get rid of a pain. And that's real. It may not be philosophic, but it's a very practical help to people when they're suffering. So I leave the question of souls to the ministers or priests or whatever. And I still say that gums are honest. They don't lie."

Again Seven just stared; he was learning more about George every minute.

George grinned and said, "You surprised? Anyhow, that's why a con game like that makes me mad—giving people false hopes. Though hell, I can understand the motives involved! I think I'll just play along to see what they plan next before I lower the boom."

"You'll have to find Gregory's twin first," Seven said.

51

"And I was thinking how great it was that the kid's attitude had changed so for the better, miracle or no," said George, starting to laugh again. "Instead—two kids. Well, the joke's on me, I guess."

But then, suddenly George's mood changed. He dug his foot into the sand beneath the swings and said, in a harder voice, "Except that it's not such a funny joke, when you come right down to it. Hell, I don't know. But I worked on that custodian's teeth the other day; he told me he was Christ, all right. He seemed like a nice enough guy. When I was finished he said, "God bless you," or something like that. . . ." George broke off, obviously embarrassed.

Seven said, "And—?"

"Shit," George went on, grinning self-deprecatingly. "But for just a few moments there I felt great, renewed, vigorous, full of life or whatever. The attendant said that kind of thing happened now and then, and laid it to suggestion. And it *had* to be—suggestion. But goddammit, I'm not particularly suggestible, or I didn't think I was.

Momentarily George seemed to forget that Seven was even there. He mused, aloud but to himself, "I thought of all kinds of things that I haven't thought about, in years . . . and now this. It's a dirty shame when people take advantage like that—"

"Like what?" Seven asked, unable to remain quiet.

"Like, well, hell, raise false hopes like that," George cried, throwing up his arms in the air. "Well, let's get going," he said. "Life's no playground, I'll tell you that. . . . And I'm going to catch that bunch red-handed."

Resolutely George got up and began striding toward the parking lot. Beside him, feeling some alarm, Oversoul Seven almost shouted, "You might be in for more surprises than you're counting on. . . ."

But George didn't answer. He was filled with righteous indignation; his brown eyes blazed, his arms swung vigorously at his sides. "A joke is a joke and enough is enough," he said. And Seven thought that George suddenly bore an uncomfortable resemblance to his grandfather, George Brainbridge the First.

Chapter Nine

George Hears
Further Disclosures:
His Dilemma Deepens

George was to meet Gregory Diggs in the center's dental office, where they'd have some privacy. Diggs was a few minutes late for their appointment, and George muttered to Seven, "Want to bet that he doesn't come? He probably guesses we're on to him. Damn! How can life get so complicated?"

"Maybe he's on the up and up though," Seven offered, grinning as if this possibility was the furthest from his mind. "After all, we didn't find records of any twin. I mean, the records the police checked couldn't have been tampered with."

"Records or no, it's the only possible explanation," George said stubbornly. "Unless you believe in miracles."

"Maybe miracles are events we just don't understand," Seven ventured. "Science admits there's lots of phenomena that can't be explained—"

"But gums are gums!" George said, as if that ended all possible discussion.

Before Seven could answer, Gregory Diggs walked in and closed the door behind him. George didn't even wait for Diggs to sit down. He advanced, demanding, "All right, where's your twin? We know you have one."

"Twin?" exclaimed Gregory, completely confused.

"The guy with the bad gums," George said, meaningfully. "There's two of you. You show me your good gums and tell me some crazy story about a healing. And I fall for it—or I almost did. We found the records of your twin," he said, lying with a sense of true virtue.

Gregory Diggs stared at George with an honest outrage that even George could see was beyond manufacture; so that George, who was basically good-hearted, felt instantly guilty.

"I don't have any goddamned twin," Gregory Diggs said, in a sputtering completely disbelieving voice. "How could you come up with *that*? I mean, maybe I haven't always played cricket with the world, but I swear I've been completely above board in all this. I tell you, the guy healed my gums. It's true, I left a few details out, but they didn't have anything to do with my gums," Gregory said, guiltily. He looked at Seven.

In some alarm, Seven said, "Forget it. Dr. Brainbridge has had enough to put up with today. I'll tell him tomorrow."

"No. I want to get it over with," Gregory Diggs insisted, sounding as stubborn as George had earlier. "I told you, I'm starting over. The world's just different for me now."

"Tell me what?" George asked, with a silly quizzical look as if not sure he wanted to know at all.

So Seven just threw up his hands, telling himself that he'd ad-lib some explanations along the way, and Gregory began, in a hesitant, somewhat defensive voice:

"This was before my gums got healed. I saw you in the morning, and you said nothing could be done for them. They hurt like hell, and I was mad. I figured like I used to, that nobody gave a damn. Anyhow that night I decided to skip town, only I didn't have any money. So I looked up your address in the phone book and went over." Diggs stopped, glanced almost imploringly at the wide-eyed George and continued, "Well, I figured on stealing some drugs and selling them on the street for cash. I figured you probably got them free anyhow. Well. . . ." He broke off, looking twice as uneasy as he had before.

"You may as well tell it all," said George. He kept shaking his head and staring inquiringly at Seven.

"Hell, I don't know," Gregory said, almost stammering. "I went inside. The downstairs was dark. A car was in the garage, and there were lights on upstairs in the back. I reckoned that the downstairs office was closed for the night. If I was quiet, I could get away with it. The back door wasn't even locked, so I went in. . . ."

"Where I found him," Oversoul Seven said briskly.

"Why didn't you tell me?" George's eyebrows leapt upward.

"Well, he didn't take anything, that's the important thing," Seven said. "We had a talk. So I didn't want him to get in more trouble than he was. . . ."

"For Christ's sake," George said.

"So when you left," Seven said, brightly, "I went downstairs to see what was going on, and found Gregory here pawing around looking for drugs."

George, looking awed, just stared at Seven. "My God, that was a brave thing to do," he said. "Dumb. But Brave."

Seven had the grace to blush, and George said, "But why? I'd have been able to handle it okay."

Seven did not answer, leaving George to figure things out for himself.

"Yeah . . .," George said, still confused.

Gregory, who had been just standing there, then said, "That isn't all, though. This last is wild."

"*This last,*" Seven was sure, was going to consist of Gregory's story about finding the gaslights turned on, the house appearing in the time of George's grandfather, and worse—of Gregory's confrontation with George the First. Seven braced himself and eyed George uneasily.

"Wild?" George thundered, sounding quite a bit like his grandfather. "That's *all* these last few days have been. Wild. So get on with it."

Gregory gulped. "Well, before Seven found me, somebody else did—a gentleman dressed in an old-fashioned red dressing gown, carrying an ancient rifle. He aimed it right at me. First, though, he switched on the lights, only they weren't electric. There were gaslights all over. I yelled I wasn't armed at all."

Silence. George's mouth dropped open. He rubbed his brow and said, "I just don't believe what I'm hearing."

"I didn't believe it either," Gregory nearly shouted. He was more and more agitated, remembering. "He sat me down and gave me a lecture, and he was a dentist, too. He put cloves on my gums. Only . . . everything looked like a movie set, like the room was out of the last century or something. I thought . . . it was some crazy relative of yours or something. He said *he* was Dr. George Brainbridge. I was trying to figure out what to do when Dr. Seven, here, came in. He yelled, and the guy in the dressing gown picked up his rifle and went upstairs. Then Seven let me go. I ran back to the psych center without being caught. The next morning, Window healed my teeth."

George Brainbridge's eyes were a study in the expression of utter amazement. He started to laugh, certain that Seven and Gregory were playing a trick. Then, staring at Gregory's obvious resoluteness, George caught back the laugh and gasped instead. "You've got to be putting me on!" he exclaimed, knowing beyond all hope that he'd heard the second most amazing story of his life—and that it was the rockbottom truth.

Seven said, "Uh, maybe Gregory was frightened and hallucinated the man with the rifle."

"*You* told him to go away," Gregory cried.

"Uh, exactly," Seven replied, redfaced.

George Brainbridge sat down, put his head in his arms and groaned. Then, lifting his head, grinning, he said, "Okay. Suppose I pretend for a minute that anything's possible. Describe the man in the dressing gown."

"He had sandy hair—bushy brows—thinnish, about six feet," Gregory said promptly. "His dressing gown was velvet—I couldn't believe it—with tassels on the belt. And wait—sure, it had a monogram, G.B."

George just stared. His face grew pale, while incongruously his grin still lasted. "My grandfather looked like that when he was alive. And he had a dressing gown like that. I remember it from when I was a kid."

Gregory stared back incredulously. "Oh no. Uh-uh. This wasn't any ghost," he said in a shaking voice. "I couldn't see through him, or anything. But he put cloves on my gums. No ghost could do *that*. I could show you where he kept them."

"There's no oil of cloves in *my* office," George said clearly. "My grandfather *was* a dentist. He used cloves. I remember the smell—"

"That's it!" Gregory cried. "The smell burnt my eyes."

"And you don't have a twin? Those were *your* gums?" George asked in a quiet voice.

Gregory nodded. "The man I saw was solid, though," he objected. "Dr. Seven saw him. And the gaslights, too."

"I've seen him before," Seven admitted, blushing. Then to George: "He *does* seem to be your grandfather."

"You too?" George shouted. "Why didn't you tell me? Never mind; you didn't think I'd believe you, I suppose. Well, I don't." He plunked down in his own dentist's chair and glanced out the small window. "At least I wouldn't have, a few days ago. I do now, though God knows why. Do either of you realize what this does to my life? My grandfather's ghost . . . and a man who thinks he's Christ healing diseased gums? What am I supposed to do with this? I ask you, quite honestly."

"Accept the events as part of reality," Seven said quickly. "Since they happened, they're legitimate, whether or not they're supposed to happen or not. You've never been a quitter."

"How do you know?" George asked, suspiciously.

"Well, you sure don't act like one," Seven amended hastily.

"You happen to be right," George replied. "And if these things happened—well, they happened. Only why to *me*, for Christ's sake?"

"What about me?" Gregory Diggs exclaimed. Then, slowly, "You know, I've done a lot of thinking lately and I might have found an answer to that, sort of."

He paused, and George said, "Well, come on, out with it. Hell, I'm really interested."

Gregory looked at the floor, then said, "Well, I'm not looking for sympathy, but my childhood was crummy. Poor. Father was a drunk. Mother not much better. Five kids. I didn't think anyone cared a shit about me; I mean nobody . . . And for a bunch of years at night sometimes I used to—I don't know how to say this—stare at the sky and think, 'You sunabitchin' universe, you could do some tiny nice thing just for me if you wanted.' I didn't care how small it was; but I wanted some tiny miracle at least that was just for me, to let me know that life or the universe or something knew I was alive. And cared."

Gregory muttered the last sentences, yet spoke them so quickly that George and Seven had difficulty understanding him. When Gregory was finished, George said, "Hell, I'm sorry. . . ."

"But don't you see?" Gregory interrupted, speaking firmly now. "I think that was it, somehow. I mean, back then I wanted a miracle so bad. So maybe it just took this long for one to catch up with me."

Forgetting himself, Seven cried, "Of course! I forgot how important *you* are in all of this. Now I see why. Your intent—"

"I wish somebody would explain it all to me," George said, interrupting. Then, to Gregory, "Gaslights, you said?"

Gregory just nodded.

"So what's to be done?" Seven asked briskly.

George Brainbridge stood up, his face full of resoluteness, his eyes narrowed with intentness, his hands on his hips. "I'm going to check out John Window," he declared. "And if he *can* heal gums or anything else, the world, or somebody should know about it. The medical society. God knows who."

"No, you can't do that," Gregory protested. "They'd make his life a living hell. You don't understand. When Window thinks he's Christ, he can heal, at least he healed me, but he's paranoid. He's afraid that . . . he'll be crucified. I mean he really gets panicky. I admit it sounds screwy, but to tell the authorities would scare Window to death."

"Well, what do you suggest, then?" George asked, exasperated. "I thought you wanted publicity."

"I don't know what to do. Nothing, maybe," Gregory said, in a subdued tone.

"And if the guy *has* been healing, say, other patients, how come it isn't out by now?" George asked.

"They're all supposed to be nutty to one extent or another," Gregory said, almost shouting. "I mean, you didn't want to believe me. Who'd believe one of the patients?"

"Yeah. Well—" George said.

"Man, I sure am sorry I said *anything,*" Gregory murmured. "I just wanted to prove you wrong in the beginning. Now I'm really sorry I did. I sure don't want to make it hard on the very guy . . . that helped me. It wasn't just my gums, you know. My whole world is better now. My whole life. . . ." He looked to be near tears.

"Look," George said, reassuringly, "I'll just talk to Window's doctor, and Window; nobody else without checking with you. Okay?"

"Yeah," Gregory said, sounding unconvinced.

"Do you trust my word?" George asked.

"Yeah," Gregory replied, surprising himself. He realized that he liked George Brainbridge, and Dr. Seven, and anyway he felt as if he'd found real friends for the first time in his life. Only—Window was a friend, too. And he wouldn't let anything hurt him.

"Of course, there's no proof that was my grandfather," George said with an embarrassed laugh. "I'm just taking you both at your word, but for the life of me I can't see why you'd want to lie. Can you describe the room?"

"I sure can," Gregory said. "It was all old-fashioned. So was the dentist's office. I mean, it had weird little wooden tables in it and lace curtains at the window, and a funny dentist's chair not like the one here at all. There was, uh, Victorian furniture, I guess you'd call it. And in particular a gigantic fern set in a pot by the window— in the dentist's office. I hid behind it, but I was caught anyway."

As evenly as he could, George said, "I have a photo in an old album of my grandfather's office, there was a plant just like that by the window." He shook his head. "This thing is beginning to make its own peculiar sense, I feel. But I can't really get a handle on it. What about you, Seven?"

"I don't believe he's a ghost," Seven replied, deciding that it was time for George to know a few more facts of life. "I think that some-how or other, when you aren't there, time changes and the past appears. Or something like that."

"You mean, I go out and close the door and bango—inside the house it's 1900 or something?"

Seven thought that George was going to snort or laugh in disbelief, but instead his face went from initial astonishment to relief.

George took his glasses off, cleaned them with a tissue, and shook his head. "I used to be afraid I was going crazy sometimes when I was a kid. Damn, I forgot the whole thing until now. Or shoved it out of my mind anyhow. I never got along with my father, but my grandfather was an idol of mine. He died when I was nine. Sometimes I thought I saw him, upstairs usually. But several times it happened in the waiting room, downstairs, in broad daylight. But as a kid com-ing down the front stairs, I had the weirdest impression that the rooms at the foot of the stairs were . . . different, and that if I was careful, I could catch them the way they were before. . . . Before what? Hell, I didn't know. But I used to sneak down the stairs at odd hours, and one night I swear I saw the waiting room as it was when my grandfather was in his prime. And there were gaslights.

As I grew up I convinced myself that it was all my imagination. . . ."

George's eyes were half closed. His voice grew dreamy. "Granpa was known as a sort of odd nut. Adored by his patients. He was the best of the Victorian do-gooders, up to his neck in humanitarian work and so forth. He left an old journal. It's in the attic somewhere, I suppose. But he was into . . . expansion of consciousness or something like that, and he followed all the works of William James. He carried on some weird experiments and wrote to James about them, I guess. My father said he was dotty and told me to rid my mind of my grandfather's nonsense." Coming back to himself, George's face reddened and he said, "So I grew up to be a good red-blooded American boy." Then, "Hell, I don't know what I'm apologizing for. I'm a damn good dentist."

"So was your grandfather," said Seven, grinning. "And when I've seen him, he's been sniffing laughing gas. . . ."

At Seven's remark, George Brainbridge leapt to his feet. "That does it," he cried. "That's a family secret. I mean, it was considered a really deep dark secret. My father told me never to speak of it. I caught Granddad sniffing laughing gas fairly often. Summers my parents went abroad; my dad was a dandy of sorts, to be frank, a social climber. We had a housekeeper, and summers I stayed home with her and my grandfather up until the year of his death. Later I went with my parents, or to summer camp. It *must* have been my grandfather you saw one way or the other; hell, he let me sniff once, too; he was fairly old by then. I had a ball."

"Then we *did* see a ghost?" Gregory Diggs asked. "Now you're putting *me* on. He was solid, I tell you."

"It must have to do with relativity," George exclaimed. "Or time-warps. That must be involved. Einstein's theory of relativity, not that I understand it. Something about time and space being relative. Anyhow, there's got to be a scientific explanation. Shit, I'm not going to take all of this lying down. I'm going to get to the bottom of it. Weren't you pretty shaken, Seven, when you saw my grandfather strolling around?"

Seven grinned. "No. I liked him. I take things as they are. That means I'm a pragmatist, doesn't it? I mean, what happens, happens. It's silly to try and pretend it away."

"Super, super," George said, in a booming voice. "My position exactly. If people don't like it, they can go to hell." But then he shook his head again. "That sounds great," he said. "Only why did this have to happen to me? It's going to be impossible to explain to

anyone else, yet we can't just ignore it. Particularly Gregory's healing
. . . I can still see those damn diseased gums as they were—and then
whammo, they're perfectly healthy. I've got to see John Window's
therapist."

"Maybe he won't let you see Window," Gregory said, almost hopefully.

But George said, "I'd like to see him stop me. Now that I'm convinced, we're going to see this thing through."

"That's what I'm afraid of," said Gregory. And Oversoul Seven
was beginning to feel the same way.

Chapter Ten

Seven and George
Meet Dr. Josephine Blithe,
and Christ Disappears

George Brainbridge felt at a definite disadvantage. For one thing, he was sweaty and hot. It was his afternoon off, but he'd already gone to the homes of two patients who couldn't get to the office, and now he was dying for a cold beer. He wore shorts and a short-sleeved sportshirt, plus the old sneakers he always put on the minute his office hours were over.

On the other hand, Dr. Josephine Blithe of the Psych Center obviously went in for appearances. Her blue summer suit was impeccably neat; her black hair didn't show a spot of perspiration at the temples, and her armpits were dry. Mentally George groaned; she was probably one of those professional women who had to prove that they *were*, well, professional. Her smile was social, polite, cool, and guarded.

"Dr. Brainbridge? Right on time," she said, with a hint of a raised eyebrow as she glanced at his rather hairy, almost but not quite pudgy, thighs. "I understand you want to discuss one of the patients, a Mr. John Window."

She hadn't said, "Sit down" yet, but George did, sitting in the upholstered chair facing her desk. He crossed his thighs, and grinned engagingly, "Now as a dentist, I know about teeth. No mystery there. The mind's something else, though. And that's your field."

"Uh, hold it," she said. "And this is?" She indicated Oversoul Seven who had entered diffidently behind George. George grinned, again engagingly. "Uh, my associate. I didn't think you'd mind, but if you do, of course. . . ." He'd asked Seven at the last moment. He still didn't know why. And Seven hadn't been included in the appointment.

Josephine Blithe stared hard at Seven, then smiled as if she meant it and said, "Okay, you can stay," and George grinned inwardly, thinking that for some damn reason, everyone seemed to like Seven. Seven just nodded politely and sat down.

Then Josephine said to George, "There's always the matter of confidentiality, of course."

"Always," George said, settling himself a bit more comfortably. Josephine seemed to shrink back slightly, a fact George noticed at once. What was the matter with her? he wondered, with slight irritation. Hadn't she seen a man in shorts before?

"The patient you're interested in is John Window. On the phone you didn't tell me anything more. So suppose you fill me in?" Josephine said in a prim, distant voice.

"Hell, I was hoping you could fill *me* in," George replied, lighting a cigarette. "I admit I'm stumped, or I wouldn't be here. This guy thinks he's Christ, right? Well, that's one thing. But I've another problem, and before I tell you about it, I'd like to ask you a few rather off-beat questions."

"Oh?" she said.

"Has this guy ever . . . healed anyone of anything? Hell, I don't know any other way to put it," George said, so embarrassed that he felt himself sweating more profusely than before.

"*Healed* anyone? Oh, that's rich." Her sudden laugh was so brittle and falsely brilliant that George almost leapt to his feet in alarm. She was terrified, the laugh told him that.

He was accustomed to people's behavior under the stress of dental work. Some laughed one moment and were hysterical the next. And Josephine Blithe was laughing that kind of laugh. But why? And

63

what was she frightened of? She caught herself, though, and went from the fake humor right into an equally fake simplistic explanation that anyone could see she didn't believe herself.

"Oh, forgive me," she said, daintily wiping away the tears of laughter with a linen handkerchief. "You've heard those delightful impossible *stories!* Honestly." She leaned forward in her chair, smiling across the desk with assumed frankness. "In a place like this, the line between fact and fiction frequently gets confused," stated Josephine in her brisk, professional manner. "People imagine things, of course. And with someone around who believes he's Christ, well, the rumors fly. Suggestion is an important *culprit* in this respect, I'm afraid. But is that why you wanted to talk about John Window? He's harmless enough, I assure you; in fact, he's a custodian here. . . ."

She was out of breath. George saw with some not unkind satisfaction that there were sweat beads above her lips. "I don't think you believe that," he said.

Her eyes flew open. They turned defiant. "I beg your pardon," she said.

Seven had purposely remained silent. Now he said, "I think George means that you're perceptive and knowledgeable enough to wonder yourself about John Window's behavior. Uh, we aren't here in any kind of official context," Seven added, in a conspiratorial tone, "We understand that you have to be careful in your capacity as psychologist here."

George shook his head. Careful about what? He wondered. What was Seven getting at? Whatever it was, Josephine Blithe certainly responded. She suddenly relaxed, and the strain went out of her shoulders. "Yes, I *do* have to be careful," she replied. "Thank you for recognizing that fact."

"I always put my foot in my mouth," said George with that self-deprecating grin. "Seven, here, is more diplomatic, I guess. So anyhow I'll put this question to you. Do you think that Window is capable of perpetrating a fraud, or taking part in a con game of any kind?"

She was honestly shocked; scandalized. "I definitely do not," she said, her voice severe again. "Now maybe you'd better tell me what you really have in mind." She half turned, glancing out the window. Then decisively she swung around again. "Well?" she demanded.

"Okay, what we have is this," George replied, staring at his hands. "I have a patient whose gums were in a state of advanced deterioration. Two days later, those same gums were perfectly healthy and the teeth were tight. The patient said that John Window healed him, here, in this institution. Now I just don't know what to do with this."

Seven said softly, "At first George thought fraud might be involved, that the one patient was actually a set of identical twins, one with good gums and one with bad. But now we understand that there *was* no fraud."

Again George shook his head. It must be the heat, he thought, because he was having trouble distinguishing Seven's words, but their tone was instantly comforting. Moreover, this reassuring effect carried over to Dr. Josephine, too, because the muscles of her face relaxed again.

"We aren't accusing Window of anything," Seven said, in that same voice. "If Window *does* have any extraordinary abilities, we thought you'd be aware of it, and George thought that this would put you in a very uneasy position."

The words were getting through to George, and he stared at Seven with abashed admiration. Seven was a natural psychologist!

So George said, "That's why we decided to bring this thing to you, rather than to anyone else."

"I knew it, I knew it would happen someday," Josephine Blithe cried. Then, in a rush, "If you knew the strain I've been under. It's a wonder *I'm* in my right mind! I knew this thing would get out sometime, that John would heal the wrong person—somebody who would talk to the authorities, or something. Actually, I guess I'm relieved. At least I can share this incredible burden with someone else." She paced the floor.

George was completely astonished. His face had a rosy, sweaty, quizzical grin. "Share what? What burden? Are you telling us that Window *does* heal? I mean, he really does this?" Now George was scandalized by the turn of events. How could an accredited psychologist say such a thing? "I thought surely you'd convince me that suggestion was somehow responsible," he said, almost shouting. "I couldn't see how on earth it could be, but I thought a psychologist would—" He stopped in mid-sentence, ashamed of himself.

Josephine Blithe moved, standing right in front of him, and said in a hard resentful voice; "You're not going to get out of this now, even if you want to, because I'm going to tell you more than you want to know."

Silence.

Dr. Josephine Blithe stood in the center of her office, staring at George Brainbridge. Her stance was alive with challenge. In the sudden quiet, bees buzzed loudly in the shrubs outside the open window, through which George saw patients and visitors walking the shaded paths. Oversoul Seven coughed.

George said, "I have the damnedest feeling that I should just get out of here while the going's good." He paused, glanced quizzically at Seven, and wiped his sweating face with a Kleenex. "What do you think, pal?" he asked.

"Why not see it through?" Seven answered, but he was uneasy on George's behalf. Besides that, he felt intriguing comprehensions skirt around the corners of his mind, but he couldn't seem to catch them.

"Well? Make up your mind," Josephine said. Her hands were on her hips, and her dark eyes were wide with either anticipation or anger, George couldn't tell which.

"Okay," he said, grinning. "I'll probably regret it, but what the hell."

With that, Dr. Blithe sat down and almost seemed to go into a reverie.

"I really don't know where to start, don't you know," she said in a soft, distant voice. "So I'll tell you about my first meeting with John Window, and fill in the details later." She raised her dark brows with a jerky, nervous motion, paused, and went on quickly as if afraid that she'd never tell the whole story unless she did it now.

"This is a small community institution. Clients get a fair amount of attention, but the emphasis is on getting the less disturbed ones into decent shape so they can get back out into the world. We have 'half-way houses' for them. Sometimes they become outpatients. But John and a few others caused no problems here; they had jobs of a kind within the institution and for various reasons, no one figured they'd be able to make it outside. So I suppose they ended up with less attention. Anyway, I'd been here several weeks before I got to check John's chart and set up an appointment.

"Well, I had a miserable migraine headache that day. I'd taken medication, but nothing seemed to help much. It was just after lunch. I felt vaguely sick to my stomach. Then John Window came for his first appointment with me. I'd read his file. Later I'll show it to you, but that doesn't matter now. Have you met him? Oh, of course, you worked on his teeth. Well, there he was, a quite ordinary man, medium everything, medium height, coloring, weight. Nothing distinctive. I found myself wondering that he was imaginative enough to ever believe he was Christ. I introduced myself. He sat where you're sitting now, Dr. Brainbridge. May I call you George?"

George nodded.

"George," she said. "Anyway, we didn't mention Christ. He said he was John Window. In my first interviews with clients, I go gently to set up a good rapport if possible, so we talked briefly about innocuous subjects. I must have glanced out the window or perhaps checked my watch, because I didn't catch the transition at all. When I looked up, well, something happened. He said, mildly enough, 'Christ, here. Now let's get rid of that headache. You see? It's quite gone.' And everything about him had changed. The very *ordinariness* of his appearance magnified, so that he seemed to represent all men. It was as if *ordinariness* was raised to an incredible degree. So that it wasn't ordinary at all, of course." (She wet her lips.) "And in that instant my headache vanished. And mind you, I hadn't even told him I had a headache."

George Brainbridge stood up and started pacing the room. Seven felt sorry for him and for Josephine Blithe, too; how difficult it must be, he thought, when you found miracles so hard to accept.

Josephine paused. Her face reddened. "I was shocked. I mean, wouldn't you think I would have been delighted first of all? But my first thought was, 'This is awful; he can't do that.' And he— John Window or Christ or whoever—smiled exactly as if he knew what I was thinking. Even as all that went through my head, though, John was John again. He seemed not to know what had happened. I thought he was pretending, but he wasn't. His face was guileless. But I was—unbelievably I guess—almost in a fury. I told him that we'd have to cut the interview short; that I'd forgotten another appointment, and I really hustled him to the door."

She stopped; out of breath. The bees in the shrubs sounded loudly again. George looked embarrassed and shook his head.

"Now *that* could have been suggestion," George said. "I don't know much about it, but aren't migraines emotionally based?"

Josephine glared at him, placed her hands on her hips and stood up, legs spread out, the tips of her summer sandals pointing in almost opposite directions. "I'm aware of the emotional aspects of migraine," she said in a cold, even voice. "And up to that point, mine had always lasted several days. I used to get them every other week or so. Well, I haven't had one since, and that was six months ago." Her voice softened. She brought her feet together almost primly and said, "I shouldn't blame you, though. I was so upset about the whole thing that I avoided John Window like the plague for a while. I kept making excuses for not seeing him until finally I couldn't stand myself, of course. . . ."

She lowered her voice again. "There are other incidents too, but for now, here are the main points. I'd be passing through the corridors and find a small group around Window, or maybe he'd be standing there with just one patient. They protect him, I've had evidence of that, I'll tell you later . . . But *some* patients that I'd worked with, without any discernible results—well, they suddenly improved remarkably well; well enough to be released. And I'd seen John talking to those same patients. I can't tell you how I knew what he was doing, but there'd be a circle of secrecy or *conspiracy* about all of them when I found them. In each case—it happened three times—John would be Christ while they talked. He reverted to Window the minute I came by, looking at me with that same damned ignorance or innocence. . . ."

"Nothing you could prove one way or the other," George muttered.

Without warning, Dr. Blithe almost bent over with laughter. Tears ran down her face. George sprang forward, wondering what the devil she was up to. Eyes half closed, she reached for her linen handkerchief. "Oh, I'm sorry. I've held all this in for so long. You understand? I haven't told anyone. But—" She looked George straight in the face for a moment before she started laughing again, and in between gasps, she cried, "*Proof?* Uh. No proof at all. But since John's been here we have one of the highest rates of cures in the East. Patients spend less time in here and are released to society far quicker than at institutions with far greater facilities and professional staffs. And . . ." Her laughing stopped at once. "Before too long, somebody's going to wonder how come."

George stared at her unbelievingly. "You're not trying to tell me that this guy . . . cures mental patients?"

She nodded vigorously. "Not only that, but embarrassingly enough, I get a good deal of the credit. I'm the only full-time psychologist in this wing of the center. We're dealing with disturbed people here, of course; the really bad cases are in another wing entirely. So we're not talking about severe psychotics."

George and Josephine had nearly forgotten Seven, as he'd hoped they would. He just sat quietly, listening, growing more amazed at human reactions with each moment. Just *why* did George and Josephine consider Window's miracles so disrupting and unwelcome?

Couldn't they see that they were manufacturing a problem where none existed? Obviously they couldn't, so somewhere he himself had failed to understand their reasoning or motivation.

If he weren't so confused about all this, Seven thought, he'd probably also know why George and Josephine were ignoring so much else that was happening around them. Like the fantastic June afternoon, in which Seven almost kept losing himself. What a delightful corner of the universe! he kept thinking, whenever he took his mind off the conversation for an instant. The air in the room smelled of the roses that climbed up the decorative iron filigrees just outside the window. The shrubs were alive with insects, bees, and birds. The damp yet sweet odor of the river swirled invisibly, and appreciating all of this, Seven almost forgot George's and Josephine's predicament.

Not for long, though. When he came to himself again, Seven saw that Josephine was near tears, though controlling herself with obvious difficulty. George stood nearby, looking concerned and embarrassed. So Seven leapt to his feet, all crisp efficiency. "This can all be figured out," he said to Dr. Blithe. "Certainly science doesn't have all the answers yet." Josephine instantly brightened, causing George Brainbridge to think, "That was exactly the thing to say." He was again astonished at Seven's sensitivity.

"I know," Josephine replied. "That's what's kept me going, of course, the chance of discovering something. . . . Perhaps some psychological mechanism that would lead to healing. And when Window thinks he's Christ, he heals. Window himself can't heal anything. So how could his obsession release abilities. . . ?" Her voice trailed off in confusion.

"You're kidding," George Brainbridge thundered. Then *he* started laughing. "I've got the solution, then. Get rid of Window's obsession, and we don't have any problems!" He grinned with feigned wickedness, leered, then added slowly, "Hey, that's not a bad idea. Could you do it?"

Oversoul Seven was so scandalized by the suggestion that he just stared at George with true horror.

"I . . . just couldn't do that," Josephine said, frowning. "I thought of it . . . of trying, I mean." She paused, threw her head back defiantly, and again her glance was full of challenge. "He *does* have some kind of healing ability. Your experience with the boy's gums proves that. What right have any of us to rob him of that, just so he'll fit into our preconceived ideas of normality? That's why I've been stymied

. . . and you're talking as if science really knew how to cure obsession."

"Yeah," George said. His face reddened. He felt ashamed of himself and at a disadvantage again. His pragmatism came to his aid: "Well, if that's what we're faced with, we may as well admit it," he said, in a hearty almost blustery way. "As long as we know our feet are on the ground. *Any* ground. Can I see this Window? I've got to start someplace."

By now Dr. Josephine Blithe looked considerably subdued. She nodded. "There's one thing, though. I want to be there, too," she said. "And we have to be very careful. When John is Christ, he's quite paranoid."

"Jesus . . ." George muttered in a long drawn-out voice.

"Wait here," Josephine directed. "I'll check and see when I can slate Window for an appointment. Actually I'm relieved. I didn't want to talk to him alone." She left the room.

George lit a cigarette and shook his head at Seven. "I just don't believe this," he said.

"Why not?" Seven asked in an oddly clear voice that somehow made George uncomfortable. Why not? He began listing all of the reasons that made the entire affair seem quite unbelievable when Dr. Josephine Blithe came hurriedly back into the room. Her face was white.

"Window isn't around anywhere," she cried. "No one's seen him since early morning."

"Jesus!" George said.

"He won't even go out on the plaza, though he's allowed to. He's too afraid of strangers," Josephine said with a very worried air. "I'll have to report this, of course. But where would he go? And why? I mean, he liked it here."

"Yeah?" George replied ironically. "Well we'd better find him fast." Without knowing exactly why, George Brainbridge was a very frightened man. He felt as if some remarkable crisis had emerged in his life, one that threatened all of his beliefs and values.

Chapter Eleven

The Museum of Time

While Oversoul Seven was concentrating on George Brainbridge's problems he was, of course, simultaneously involved with all of his other personalities as well. Since he had a body to contend with, too, this demanded a multiplication of focuses that Seven was still in the process of perfecting. He was also having experiences with his teacher, Cyprus, who was monitoring his actions from her own impeccable viewpoint.

For example, even as George Brainbridge was saying to Dr. Josephine Blithe, "Maybe we can find John Window before anyone realizes he's missing," Oversoul Seven suddenly heard Cyprus' voice; and when he did, he managed to stay in Josephine's office (nodding his head, he hoped, in the right places) while his main consciousness formed a small bit of light that played on the ceiling. Cyprus was another spot of light, dancing at the top of the window.

"None of this will do at all," Cyprus said. She moved at the speed of light, of course, as did Seven, so their conversation took hardly any time at all.

"I know it won't do," Seven cried. "Where have you been? Just tell me where Window is, that's all, and I'll straighten things out somehow."

Cyprus sighed. "You *know* I can't tell you," she said. "That would be cheating—"

"So cheat," Seven replied. "Look at George. He's half out of his mind. He doesn't even understand miracles."

Cyprus smiled, looking down at the rumpled George, who was wiping the perspiration from his face and saying, "I bet that damn Gregory Diggs took Window somewhere to protect him."

The physical Seven nodded vigorously, yet to Cyprus's and Seven's consciousnesses, the motions and sounds of the room were incredibly slow.

"But why?" Josephine asked.

"I see what you mean," Cyprus said sympathetically. "I'll give you some hints. First, remember the message you received earlier about the Codicils. They're vitally important. And remember that all of your personalities are involved in one way or another with the activities of any *one* of them. And in earth terms of course, you *do* have a deadline."

"A deadline?" Seven asked, more uneasy than ever.

"Oh, Seven, just find Window," Cyprus said, softly. "I'll give you another clue; follow your impulses. And in physical terms, hurry! You *do* know where he is."

"I do?" Seven said, wonderingly. But instantly he was fully back in his body, which George Brainbridge was nudging with his elbow.

"Come on, let's get going," George demanded.

Almost teetering on her high-heeled sandals, Josephine Blithe said, with bitter amusement, "Yeah, we're off to see the Wizard of Oz."

"Super," Seven said, complimenting himself on making a suitable reply under somewhat confusing conditions.

The conditions became even more confused—and disorganized, Seven thought, as the afternoon progressed. First they searched the Psych Center—as nonchalantly as possible—for Window or for Gregory Diggs. When this failed, they all piled into George's Porsche and began driving up and down the streets in the hopes of sighting one or the other.

"If we drive up and down past this shopping center one more time, I'll go crazy," Josephine said finally. "We've been everywhere around town with no sign of either of them. For all we know, they're on a bus to Timbuktu or somewhere. We don't even know for sure if they're together." She sighed. Her makeup was caking from the heat; her shoes hurt, and she didn't like being crowded so close to George Brainbridge in the car's front seat.

From the small back seat, Seven said, "Let's park and talk a minute. Maybe we can think of a plan of action. Park in front of your place, George, why don't you? Where it's cool." Seven didn't know why he mentioned parking in front of George's, but the minute he did, he remembered the odd time-transfers that had happened in the spot where George's house stood. Follow your impulses, Cyprus had said. Was that what she meant?

"It's okay with me," George replied with weary resignation.

Josephine eased one shoe off and rubbed one heel with the other one. They pulled up in front of George's house. "I don't see the point of this," Josephine said with a worried air. "We're just not getting anyplace."

Seven was tempted to agree.

"Hell, we'll find him sometime," George replied, without conviction. "If he's in town, that is."

But Seven was suddenly alert; George's words made brilliant sense—"We'll find him some*time*"—Seven thought. Of course!

"Your car windows need a good washing," Josephine said for something to say, and Seven stared at her. Did she realize what else her words meant besides what they were saying? Probably not. But when Josephine said the word "windows" Seven was suddenly reminded of someone he'd entirely forgotten. ("Well, not entirely of course," he said later to Cyprus.) He remembered another man, one whose name was Window—a personality of his, who was in the twenty-third century, the last time Seven checked. And John Window was like an unclear version of the twenty-third-century Window. He was, Seven thought with sudden inspiration, like a window that needed cleaning because it was distorting a view. . . .

"Yeah, I know. I'll clean 'em before Jean comes home," George said. "She always complains about that, too."

In that moment Seven knew that something was going to happen, and he didn't want George or Josephine around when it did. On impulse, he opened the car door and squeezed himself out. "I think I'll sit on the porch a while," he said, a bit apologetically. "The heat's really getting to me. It's getting toward suppertime, but I'm not even hungry. Why don't you two get a bite and pick me up afterward? In the meantime, 'I'll think a lot,' " he said, borrowing one of George's pet phrases.

Josephine shook her head. "No food for me. But I think we should check the center again. George can look outside, and I'll go in on some pretext or other. . . ."

Seven nodded impatiently because he could already feel times changing. The car turned the corner just as the road itself disappeared.

Seven sprang to his feet, as the house behind him disappeared; so did just about everything else. In a bewildering display, objects again appeared, disappeared, and were replaced by others.

Finally Seven remembered a knack of dealing with such events, one that he'd learned (somewhere? when?) and forgotten. He stared directly ahead, and when the next object—a small tree—appeared there, Seven kept his gaze riveted on the spot. Everything disappeared again, and now the tree was taller. So he was going into the future; at least he had *that* settled, he thought. And he wanted to find Window of the twenty-third century to see what connections there were between him and his namesake in the twentieth century. If he found the future Window . . . would he automatically find the twentieth-century one?

Seven was blinking furiously. The tree was full-grown, then dead; then the spot was vacant. A hut appeared, then the spot was empty again. Then new growth . . . Seven groaned; the spot looked more or less the way it had when he'd found himself in the twenty-fifth century with the floating cities. If so, he'd gone two centuries too far. But before he could think of anything to do about this, the environment began to stabilize. He looked up, his suspicions confirmed. The landscape looked more or less deserted, and in the sky the floating cities caught the rays of the sun like glittering, round kites.

Seven gulped; something decidedly unpleasant had happened in this latest time change. Instead of grass, the ground was covered with a sickly brown layer of vegetation that almost looked like the thin wisps of hair on a bald man's head. And beneath, the ground was almost grey in color. The only trees were dwarfed crooked ones, hardly three feet tall at most; and though the air was warm enough (meaning it was still summer), there were no flowers or birds or—

74

Seven listened intently—or insects; or if there were, they were ominously still.

As he looked about, Oversoul Seven felt a deepening sense of desolation. Here, in the very spot where George Brainbridge's house stood in easy hearing distance of the busy traffic of Water Street; where the busy twentieth-century air was full of activity—now, in the twenty-fifth century, all of that had vanished; the Earth for all purposes was a deserted, sterile world. Seven let his consciousness roam. While he stood disconsolately, his mind traveled over the nearly blank landscape. In the flash of a human eye, Seven's consciousness leapt from continent to continent. Even the seas were sluggish, and the vegetation had sloughed off the mountains so that only here or there one lonely dwarfed tree remained. What had happened?

Seven was almost overwhelmed by the desolation; he was an Earth soul after all. So what if some mortals dwelled in the manufactured cities above the earth? What heritages had been lost? What physical echoes no longer sounded in the blood?

Window wouldn't be found here, Seven realized suddenly. This world had no inhabitants. Then where was the precise future probability that Window belonged in? Besides, wasn't Window in the twenty-third century, not the twenty-fifth?

Then why had he come *here?* Seven wondered. Cyprus, he knew, would say, "Trust yourself, even your seeming mistakes." But what good would *that* do? Seven nervously looked around again. He wanted to get out of *this* probability as quickly as possible. But maybe the century was somehow right, even though he was positive that Window had been in the twenty-third century last time he remembered.

Scowling, Seven stared directly before him again, this time at a spindly, dead grey twig. Probabilities, he knew, were like tangents out from a certain time . . . they were horizontal extensions, sort of. So he stared at the twig and stared and stared. Finally it began to blur just a bit. At the same time, he felt as if he were just looking through his right eye, or tipping very gently sidewards to the right, or leaning psychologically to the right. At least this is how he tried to explain it to himself as everything—ground, sky, Seven, and all his thoughts—suddenly took a turn in one probability and shifted into another. The time was still the twenty-fifth century, for the three floating cities still hung in the sky. The twig (or its double? or triple?) was now infinitesimally to the right of the first one. The distance was so small it could never be physically measured. But Seven knew he was in a different world.

This became apparent at once as new objects kept appearing everywhere, so quickly that Seven leapt back. When he did, something struck his leg or his leg struck something, and he spun around, rubbing his eyes with momentary disbelief.

There stood what looked at first to be George Brainbridge's house in the twentieth century, and what he'd brushed up against was the hitching post that George had kept from his grandfather's time, as a decoration. Only now, it was to the right of the porch, just by the steps, instead of out by the curb. The house itself was even more confusing for it resembled George's so completely, and yet glaring distortions or differences were everywhere. It looked to be of brick, yet at the same time, it appeared to be made of some much lighter material. The three windows were right in the front waiting room, but there were also three windows on the left side, where Seven was sure George's house had only two. Besides that, though, *this* house looked newly constructed, or too good to be true, or somehow unused.

Seven stepped back to get a better look, and then saw the neat sign. It read: "The Ancient House of Many Windows: believed to be a perfect replica of a structure that actually stood in this spot roughly from 1860 to 2010. The original tell, explored in the twenty-third century, delivered artifacts that led historical designers to begin their detailed assessment of the structure. Later excavations gave further data. The discovery of the *original* Codicils was made only five years ago when an ancient bomb shelter was evacuated at a deeper level. This peoples' museum is open to the public. Further information on the Codicils inside."

The Codicils? Seven could hardly contain his excitement. Yet he was uneasy because no one was about. He sat down on the steps, looking toward the river.

The riverbank had changed; the old dikes built in George's time were now buried under new topsoil. The river must have flooded many times and then widened somehow, for now it ran deeper and wider below a high bank of planted shrubbery and trees. Seven saw no roads, only natural, well-tended paths, and he realized that he was in the middle of a park area. The surroundings were so pleasant that he was almost tempted to walk down to the river, but he sighed, and walked up the steps to the museum's porch.

Hesitantly he opened the front door. It was far lighter in weight than George's twentieth-century door, even though the material looked the same. No sooner had the door opened and Seven glimpsed the layout of the rooms off the hall, than a man's figure appeared coming down the front stairwell.

"Good afternoon," the man said. "You've missed the tour scheduled for the past hour. I can give you a private tour, however, although it won't be as extensive as the group one. Will you follow me, please?"

Seven was confused, at least momentarily. The man vaguely reminded him of the twenty-third-century Window, with his long, severe nose and intent eyes. But there was no consciousness involved at all with this figure, even though it was three-dimensional.

Before Seven could comment, the man came closer, turned in a graceful circle so that Seven could see his back, faced Seven again and said with quiet authority, "I am Monarch, appearing as a hologram and acting as your guide."

"A hologram! I should have known at once," Seven said. It was impossible not to admire the hologram: the skin, hair, eyes—everything in fact—was perfect, and the illusion of depth was flawless. Seeing Monarch's face (or rather, the image of it), Seven was almost certain that the hologram's original was also Window of the twenty-third century. Not that the features were the same, but that Seven kept seeing Window's features superimposed over the hologram's.

When Seven didn't move to follow him, the hologram-man said, "Have you a question? Technology has advanced so that I can answer almost any question that a tourist might ask, though—"

"Where is the real Window, I mean Monarch?"

"In his study. He's the force behind the evacuations and the construction of this museum. Appointments may be arranged. His administration building is a mile away, taking the western footpath which is clearly marked. Now, if you'll step into the next room, this, it is believed, was an ancient dentist's office—"

Seven took one startled glance at the open doorway through which he saw what was supposed to be a reconstructed version of George's dentist's chair. At once he saw that it was the mismatched combination of such chairs from at least four different historical periods, all put together in one. Just inside the door was a table bearing dental tools from both the nineteenth and twentieth centuries, and the label by them read: "Dental instruments."

Seven paused. "Sir?" said the hologram-man.

"I haven't time for a tour," Seven said impatiently. "I have to find Window. Uh, thanks for your attention. Super."

"I beg your pardon?" said the hologram-man. "I'm not familiar with the meaning of the last term in that context . . ." But Seven was gone, and when the door closed, the hologram-man was deactivated as the laser beams that formed his image disappeared.

As he left the museum, Seven wondered if he should have found out what the Codicils were. He knew Cyprus had said that they were vitally important. But it was imperative that he find John Window. And if he was right—a big if, Seven reminded himself—then *maybe* Window (or Monarch) in this future probability would somehow help him find the twentieth-century Window.

Seven found the western path with no difficulty. As he walked along as fast as he could, he couldn't forget that this same spot of footpaths and tall shady trees existed in the space where Water Street and Walnut Street intersected. No, he realized: in the twentieth-century reality, he would have already turned and walked up Walnut Street. And somewhere in that area, George Brainbridge and Dr. Josephine Blithe were cruising around in George's car, looking for John Window.

Seven hoped he kept the whole thing straight. He could hear himself later telling Cyprus that this had been the most complicated venture she'd ever sent him on. The fantasy in his mind faded, though, as he finally approached a large stone building with many verandas. Seven shook his head . . . this was a beautiful but hardly faithful replica of the old Christian Science church that sat on the corner of Church and Walnut Streets in George's time. A small plaque read: "Administration Building."

Was Window—Seven caught himself—Monarch inside? There was only one way to find out. Seven walked up the steps . . . and the door automatically opened.

As Seven stepped over the doorsill, he saw Monarch sitting at the end of a long, wide corridor. Seven quickly recognized him as the model of the hologram-man. But more than that, Seven's consciousness merged at once with Monarch's and, joyfully, Seven realized that Monarch and Window *were* the same and yet different. They were counterparts of each other, living in different times and yet more connected than brothers. And that meant . . . of course! Seven thought. John Window was also one of *his own* personalities, a counterpart of the others—and he had let himself forget these connections so that the various personalities would be free to seek their own ways unless or until they needed his help. And now they did.

But as soon as Seven recognized Monarch as the twenty-fifth-century Window and made other connections—and even as Monarch

78

looked up with a glance of polite inquiry—the objects and space itself began to shimmer again, wrinkle into itself, blink off and on until, blinking himself, Seven found himself standing inside the twentieth-century Christian Science church, in the reading room, staring at a startled John Window and Gregory Diggs.

"How on earth did you find us *here?* I've never even been in a church in my life before," Gregory Diggs said, as Seven appeared in the doorway.

"It's a long story," Seven replied. He felt relieved, surprised, and out of breath.

"Verily," Window replied.

"He's Christ again," Gregory said, "and I'm going to see that nobody takes advantage of him."

Seven shook his head. It was still hot, and his polyester suit wasn't even wrinkled. "What *are* you doing here?" he asked.

Diggs scowled defensively. "I'm showing Christ here that some people believe that healing is natural. He doesn't have to be afraid either because . . . well, these people say there isn't no evil either. They left bulletins at the center, so I thought we'd see what they had to offer. Nobody's going to crucify you either, because. . . ." Diggs said this last to John Window, who now believed he was Christ again. And Window stared sorrowfully at Oversoul Seven and said, "Are you Judas? Have you come to betray me?"

"Jesus Christ," Diggs said under his breath, to Seven. "Now see what you've done! Will you get out of here?"

"Hurry. Run to the door and drag Window with you," Seven cried. "If my deductions are right, George's car should be passing this place right now."

Diggs, grunting, pushed the unhappy John Window to the door. Seven threw it open. And George's car was right out front—in the very spot where Monarch's door opened in the twenty-fifth century.

Josephine saw the trio at once and told George to stop the car. They all piled in and drove off.

Chapter Twelve

Window Speaks for Monarch, and Seven Is Worried

Window, who still thought he was Christ, kept
staring sadly at George and asking, "Are you Judas?" even
as Seven hustled him and Gregory Diggs into the small sportscar.

"No he's a friend," Gregory kept repeating each time Window
asked. They were all crowded in the car together. Josephine wrinkled
her nose at George's hairy and sweaty thighs and yelled over the
sound of the motor: "I borrowed John's files." She waved a folder.

The car windows were all open, but it was still stifling. George
looked anxious. Window's Christ face was calm but resigned. George
started driving up Church Street and asked rhetorically, "Well, what
now?"

"Let's eat," Seven said. "Why not give Window a good meal in a restaurant? He missed supper at the Center, didn't he? And then we can figure out what to do next."

"I don't know," Josephine said dubiously.

"Why not?" Gregory demanded. "He could stand a treat. He's not going to embarrass anyone, if that's what you're afraid of."

"Yeah. What the hell," George said, grinning. "I've never had dinner with Christ before."

Josephine glared at him. Seven grinned. Window in his Christ voice said, "I hope it's not the Last Supper. It's not easy being Christ in this day and age."

"You just think you're Christ," Gregory said reproachfully. "I thought we settled that when we had our talk."

"Well, that isn't easy, either," Window said, intelligently enough, Seven thought. "You all eat," Window continued, cordially. "I'm fasting."

George was relieved when everyone decided on the next restaurant they came to. He was tired, wondering what on earth he was getting into, and John Window disconcerted him. For one thing, Window looked innocuous enough, and George had rather expected a more wild-eyed man, even though in the dentist's chair he'd been mild enough. But George hadn't heard of the healing then, and knowing about it now made him expect Window to demonstrate some bizarre behavior. (Damn, he thought, anybody could *say* he was Christ. If Window believed it, why didn't he do something now while George had his eye on him?)

They filed into the restaurant. The minute they sat down, they were all gripped by an air of expectancy—all but Window, who smiled amiably and said to Gregory Diggs: "I knew taking me away from the Center wouldn't work; that they'd find us."

"Yeah," Diggs replied, dourly.

"Let's decide on dinner and then talk," Seven said, with a brisk smile, because he was uneasy himself and wanted to discover why before anything happened that he couldn't control.

They were silent, reading their menus. The restaurant was quiet, with only a few patrons. "It's quiet in all the local restaurants," George said, too loudly. "Everybody's at their cottages."

Josephine Blithe ignored the statement, wet her lips, smiled earnestly, and said to Window, "John, do you believe you're Christ right now?"

"*John?*" George muttered; grinning suddenly.

"Of course, John, no need for formality. We're friends aren't we, John? You remember, we've talked before."

And suddenly, with Josephine's question, the area of interest shifted to John Window. He had the floor and he knew it. He even smiled in acknowledgment. Until this point, he had been almost unreal to them, hardly a person at all. ("In a funny fashion, he seemed almost anonymous, particularly for someone causing so much fuss," Seven told Cyprus later. And she replied, "Of course. It's too bad you didn't understand why, then.")

"Verily," John Window said, "I'm John Window who thinks he's Christ. Or I'm Christ who thinks he's John Window. This *is* a dilemma to me and, I understand, to others. I am a man of strange education; that is, what I've learned seems to have been taught to me someplace else. And I am quite articulate. Gregory has taught me to come out of the closet, as they say; I've been a closet Christ. Or a closet John Window. I'm not sure which. Does any of this answer any of your questions?" He started to eat his meal. He'd ordered fish and chips after Gregory talked him into fasting tomorrow instead.

Dr. Josephine Blithe smiled professionally. "You're doing fine, just fine," she said.

George was quite taken aback. "You don't sound crazy to me," he said. "You sure as hell sound strange. But you make it sound as if there's sense there someplace."

"I've considered all of this often," Window said, looking at George. "It's a peculiar position to be in particularly since I think that Christianity has done as much harm as good. It's seen its time. So why would anyone want to be Christ in this day and age?"

"You tell me," George said, a trifle embarrassed. Window's eyes never left George's face. Finally George blew his nose.

They'd all heard John Window speak at least briefly before, but now all of them at the same time were struck by a clear transparent quality in his voice, as if each word he spoke was somehow inevitable, and meant for them alone. Josephine struggled to maintain her professional, superior stance. "*Very* good, John," she said, in a condescending voice.

George muttered, "Damn."

Gregory Diggs said to all of them, "What did I tell you?"

John Window wore jeans, a sportshirt, and sandals. George stared at him: He didn't look any different from any other male in the room. Indeed, looking at the male patrons, then back to Window, George had the weird feeling that something in each of the other men's faces was somehow reflected in Window's. Yet Window had his own features; light blue eyes, medium complexion, rather thinnish lips; and the proportions were all normal. Yet granting this, George thought stubbornly, Window's face still had a quality he'd never seen before—and that was why he couldn't get a handle on it.

Window was saying, "I know when I think I'm Window, and I know when I think I'm Christ. What really gets me thinking, though, is this: Who is the me that thinks I'm either Christ or Window?"

"Probing question, John!" Josephine said in a bubbling voice. But it was no use to pretend; whoever or whatever he was, John Window was beyond today's psychology. It couldn't explain him. She frowned. Something else was odd, too. They'd finished their suppers. Usually a waitress would come over, but their table seemed isolated in some fashion that she couldn't explain. She almost wanted to pinch the table to see if it was alive.

"Another thing," Window said. "Christ is able to heal people— but he's paranoid. He really believes he'll be crucified. Window can't heal, but he knows that somehow he has access to that ability through Christ. And Window is sane enough. He's scared, but he isn't para-noid."

"Who's speaking now?" Oversoul Seven asked quickly before any-one could interrupt. "You spoke of Christ *and* Window. So who are *you?*"

Complete silence. George held his breath. Josephine nervously scratched her stockinged leg. Window-Christ looked the most aston-ished of any of them. He started to speak, faltered, began again. "I'm not sure. I think my name is Monarch. Or I think it could be. Now and then I think to myself as this person."

Monarch? Seven gulped. Of course. It was possible that, with psy-chological bleedthroughs, such a thing could happen. Josephine opened her mouth to speak, and Seven's suddenly commanding glance stopped her. He said, "All right, Monarch, can you help Window or Christ?"

George and Gregory Diggs were so fascinated that they couldn't take their eyes from Window's face.

George muttered, "You mean he's somebody else, *too?*"

"Shush," said Gregory, urgently. "Listen."

"I *am* Window and Christ," Monarch said, in a distant voice. And suddenly Window's face did have a "someplace else" look. "Or I was. Christ is a Window who heals." Now the voice was hesitant, as if the words were coming from far away and had to be translated; and yet, again, each individual word was clear and oddly transparent—so transparent, Seven thought (too late), that they could all fall through the voice if they didn't watch out.

No one was completely sure exactly what happened next, although Seven had a very good idea, but it was one that even he had trouble accepting.

First of all, there were changes in perception. The things in the environment remained the same. Yet to George, Josephine, Gregory and Seven, each detail in the restaurant seemed suddenly more emphatic, more itself, brighter, more separate on the one hand, yet impossibly more a part of the entire environment. George happened to be looking at a glass sugar bowl, for example, and his eyes widened as it seemed to attain a different reality than it had only the moment before. The sugar glistened—tiny dazzling crystals, each individual and somehow perfect, mixed in with each other; each crystal touching another, flowing into another while retaining its own sparkling apartness. Besides this, the reflections on the sugar bowl itself became almost dazzling, seeming to belong to the bowl, to stain the glass, while simultaneously dancing above or even within it. George felt as if he were being hypnotized.

Diggs had been looking at the toe of his right shoe. Suddenly he saw it as he never had before, as if it was the most significant thing in the world, simply because it existed. The shoe seemed planted in time, in space, solid leather resting on the wooden floor. Yet it also seemed composed of thousands of specks of light, each separate yet making up the entire structure; lights interlacing and dancing within themselves, and moving with the reflections from the restaurant lights, which also seemed somehow to belong to the shoe.

Josephine's eyes had been on an edge of a menu sticking out between a napkin holder and a ketchup dispenser. Before she realized what was happening, the letters on the menu seemed to leap upward, almost as if they were written in the air above the paper. She even swore that she saw shadows fall behind the letters for an instant, before the perspective of the entire menu changed. That is, the menu now appeared to form itself about the letters so that the word *bacon* not only seemed alive in the strangest fashion, but seemed to form the rest of the menu around itself. Each word made the menu pucker or change, as in turn each word became prominent and the others faded from view almost completely. Then—she gasped—all the words came into prominence at once, so vividly that she could hardly bear to look, and each word had a hand in forming the menu upon which it was written.

George Brainbridge had been staring rather impolitely at the spot in the front of John Window's mouth where he'd removed the bad tooth. The gap was quite noticeable, and George was idly thinking that after he took out the one beside it, he'd fit Window with a bridge. Just about then, his eye roamed toward a good tooth on the other side of the gap in Window's mouth, and what happened next left George literally breathless. ("I almost peed in my pants," he said later to Josephine, who wrinkled her lips distastefully.)

That one tooth instantly took all of George's attention. He felt the life of the roots beneath, of the nerves, the rich bed of the gums, but more . . . the tooth seemed to form the gums as much as the other way around. No, that wasn't it, he thought, struggling to understand. It was as if the tooth had a part in forming the gums that would later hold it so snugly . . . as if ahead of time the tooth, knowing its reality, demanded a mouth to hold it.

All of these changes began as the man who now called himself Monarch said, "Christ is a Window who heals." And to Seven, it was as if the man had two sets of eyes, or rather, double vision. Seven saw the restaurant, precise and definite, yet the effect was as if he were looking through the small end of a telescope—one that probed into time instead of space. At the other wide end, the full-sized, flesh-and-blood Monarch of the twenty-fifth century looked out at the expanse of landscape outside the museum; he was talking to himself. Except that it was John Window's "Monarch" in the restaurant who spoke the actual words Seven heard:

"How strange to find myself in such a place and time! I feel that I lived in Christ's era and in the twentieth century and in the twenty-fifth all at once, as if I'm a set of different selves, but with one slightly out of focus. I wonder how many other people have felt this way?"

A pause. Through the double vision that Seven saw in Window's eyes, he saw Monarch smile, just as Window's seemingly miniature face did at the same time. "Maybe Monarch is a future self to other portions of my entire selfhood. Maybe Christ and Window made my existence possible."

"And vice versa," Seven whispered, wondering if both or only one Monarch would hear him.

"Of course," said "Monarch" in the restaurant, mouthing the words of the twenty-fifth-century Monarch who now mused to himself, "Perhaps I even had a hand in initiating the Codicils that I uncovered in my own time."

"The Codicils," Seven said urgently. "Quickly, tell me about them."

"They're the basis of our civilization. Without them, the world would never have survived," mused Monarch in front of the museum, as "Monarch" in the restaurant spoke the words.

A feeling of panic almost washed over Seven as he saw the implications of Monarch's answer. He asked quickly, "When? When did they originate?"

The answer came: "In the time of 'The George.'"

With those words, the alterations of perception vanished. John Window said, "I forgot what I was doing."

George Brainbridge just shook his head and muttered, "What the hell just happened?" He was staring at Window's mouth, which now appeared quite normal.

"I don't know," said Josephine, blinking at the menu which also looked quite ordinary now. And Gregory Diggs shook his head wonderingly as the tip of his shoe lost its magic.

Window thought he was Christ again. He said morosely, "This could be a modern version of the Last Supper, don't you know? I know you're my dentist, Dr. Brainbridge. But are you certain you're not Judas too?"

"Now cut that out," George muttered, but softly, not wanting to make a scene, "I'm sure. Take my word for it, will you?"

"Verily," Christ said.

"Super," George replied, with a sigh.

"Do you remember saying you were Monarch?" Seven asked. He tried not to look worried, but he had an idea that there were more time bleed-throughs than he knew what to do with, and he wanted to question Window or Christ or Monarch while he still could.

"I think Window must be a catalyst of some kind," Josephine said to George. "I've got to tell you what just happened to me."

"Ditto," George said. "I mean, you won't believe—"

"Window, did you do something to my shoe just now?" Gregory Diggs asked.

Seven tried to cut in on the conversation, or rather to put a temporary end to it so he could question Window, but Window promptly answered Gregory. "No, you just saw it the way it is," he said, almost apologetically. "Things were complicated enough. I mean, they are. But sometimes I think I'm a future man named Monarch. When I think I'm him, people sometimes see things as they really *are*. Sometimes," he said slowly, "I suspect I have to go beyond Christ to something else."

"But you should have said something," Josephine said. "I'd have, uh, understood. Honestly, John." She reached over and touched his hand.

Window looked momentarily disconcerted. He lifted his other hand in the air, as if unsure what to do with it, then he gently placed it quickly and lightly on top of Josephine's. Her face got so red that George thought she'd suddenly developed a fever. She gave a funny muffled gasp, pulled her hand back, and just stared at Window, who said, "I was just trying to help."

"Well, I don't need your help," she whispered fiercely. "*Now* what the hell is going on?" George asked.

"Touch fire and you get burned," Gregory Diggs replied, grinning, but good-naturedly.

"Now do you see?" Window said. "I've hurt her feelings. That's another thing. Sometimes when I touch people, they touch themselves or get in touch with themselves, and it makes them angry. And I never know when that's going to happen."

Josephine grabbed her white-beaded pocketbook, sprang to her feet, and walked as quickly as she could to the door. It was obvious that she was holding back tears. George Brainbridge, looking bewildered, followed her. "Now what?" he said, as she opened the door.

She leaned against the outside of the building, dabbing at her eyes with a handkerchief. "He just did it again," she gasped. "Only this time, well, he . . . picked up a secret of mine, and told me not to worry about it. . . ."

"But he didn't *say* anything," George protested. "Just touched your hand."

"Yeah? Well, that was enough," she said, in an almost harsh voice, abandoning her lady-like manner. George grinned. "And there's more. What are we going to do with him? I'm humiliated. I've learned more about him tonight than I have in our three official appointments. And I can *see* now how I put him down . . . and programmed him to say what I wanted. George—he isn't crazy! *That's* what frightens me. And I could tell when he touched me—he was . . . sorry for *me* for not knowing how to handle it all; for being scared when he healed me of that damn headache."

"Uh. I'd forgotten that part," George admitted. "What the hell, though, that was super."

"Gregory thinks that about his gums, too. But it makes me nervous.

If someone can heal you—well, they must have some kind of power over you, mustn't they? *That* scares me too."

"Come on! Healing a headache can't be all that bad," George said, jokingly. Then with a playful leer: "What's the secret he discovered?"

"It isn't funny," she said glumly. "And something else. He's only been at the Center three months, since I was appointed. His records say he committed himself. His parents are dead. I don't know where he came from, what section of the country or anything. I just think it's damn weird."

They stood in the summer night darkness, watching the traffic speed by the parking lot. The air was somewhat cooler; Josephine pulled her summer jacket tighter, and George's legs were getting goose pimples, the tiny hairs sticking up like wires. "Damn, I'm getting chilly," he said. "I don't know what the hell to do with Window. We have to get him back before eleven, though, didn't you say?"

Josephine blushed. "Actually, I signed him out as a guest at your place to cover his absence," she said. "I mean, he's a man . . . I didn't want to sign him out to my place, because people might talk."

"You're devious," George said, grinning. "What are you saying? We should take him to my place? I mean, we're covered."

She nodded.

"I hope Jean doesn't decide to surprise me, and show up. The fewer who know about this, the better," replied George, looking worried.

"You mean, you haven't told your wife?" Josephine asked, disapprovingly.

"Told her? Hell, I haven't seen her in three days. She and the kids are at the cottage," George answered. His eyes widened. For the first time he found himself wondering about that old arrangement. "They go every summer," he said, almost defensively.

In his mind's eye he saw his wife's face, and at the same time he was uncomfortably aware of his growing pleasure with Josephine Blithe's company. "Uh. We better go get the others and get out of here, then."

"Mmm," she answered. "There's something else. I don't know what happened to you in there, but I had some changes in perception that I'd assign to drugs, except that I didn't have any. God, my peers would think I was out of my mind if they heard this!"

"Peer power, huh?" George replied, but he was growing more aware of her closeness, so he swung around almost brusquely and opened the door.

Seven's face told George that something was happening; he'd never seen Seven look so serious before. Gregory Diggs was obviously listening intently to whatever was going on. George pulled out Josephine's chair for her (for the first time) and sat down himself.

Gregory Diggs whispered, "Window is Monarch again. It's wild. Listen."

Window, as Monarch, had a bemused expression on his face. He looked at Seven and looked *through* him at the same time, as if caught up in a spectacular daydream. The twenty-fifth-century Monarch began to stroll in the direction of the museum. He felt an odd disquiet. He wondered, for the hundredth time, what had given him the idea to dig at this particular tell in the first place. And as he thought, Window as Monarch spoke the words, in the restaurant: "I wonder what actually gave me the idea for digging at this particular tell to begin with?"

"What's he talking about?" George asked Gregory. Diggs shushed him. In the background, a waitress was clearing the tables, and George leaned closer so that he could hear better.

"The Codicils' origin could have remained a mystery," Monarch mused, growing still more uneasy. "Or worse, I suppose they could have never been discovered. But what about our world, then? Without the Codicils, God knows what fate would have befallen the species." And again, in the restaurant, his eyes looking nowhere, Window as Monarch spoke the same words.

Then his words suddenly became urgent. "I've got to check the Codicils again. I don't know why," Monarch said, and he began walking as quickly as he could toward the museum. Even the Monarch speaking to Oversoul Seven grew agitated—And so did Seven. The museum in the twenty-fifth century correlated with George's house. Seven knew that he had to go there right away—and that Window had to go with him.

"It's all right," Seven said, to Window, who now was silent. "We'll work it all out. We have to."

"Work what out?" asked George, sounding irritated.

Seven had been concentrating on "Monarch's" words so intently that he hadn't even realized that George and Josephine had returned. Now he looked up at them all in sudden dismay. How could he explain what he'd just learned? What delightful human companions they were—he looked at them with a fondness that surfaced so surely that its expression was obvious. George looked embarrassed. Gregory somehow understood. Josephine blushed. But the expression of such emotion frightened George, so he said, alarmed, "What's wrong?"

"Not a thing," Seven said briskly. "Only we have to go back to your house. Quickly. I'll explain later. Right now we haven't any time to lose."

George shrugged and said, "Lead on: Nothing would surprise me now." Josephine picked up her purse. Diggs took Window's arm protectively, and, though he was still trying to look unperturbed, Oversoul Seven was almost beside himself with worry. If they didn't find the Codicils in time, this world of Josephine's, George's, Gregory's and Window's might not exist at all—or it might turn into another probability, or lead to a future probable world in which the earth lay in ruins and Monarch himself did not exist.

Window walked along docilely enough. But would he be strong enough, Seven wondered, to do what must be done?

All of Seven's sense of urgency couldn't keep the group together much longer, though. Josephine Blithe insisted they rest for a while. She went home in a taxi.

George took everyone else to his place. He went to his bedroom purposefully. Oversoul Seven fidgeted and waited while Diggs and Window drank coffee in the kitchen. So everything was quiet. But not for long.

Chapter Thirteen

A Complicated
Out-of-Body Experience
and a Full House

_____

While George Brainbridge the Third slept and
Seven talked to Window and Diggs in the twentieth-
century kitchen, George Brainbridge the First sat in his red silk dressing gown on the side of his cot, looking out the attic window at
the carriage house and drive and lawn below. His mind felt deliciously
clear and unruffled—as still, he thought, as the June night sky whose
moonlight illuminated the scene outside his window with such deli-
cate artistry. He was trying to get out of his body.

It's 1892, he told himself. And no matter how definite and authorita-
tive that date sounded to him, no matter how perfectly his sense
data confirmed it, he had to try to realize that other times—other
years, seasons, and even centuries, somehow coincided in this moment.
He *had* learned that much. And, he reminded himself, no matter

that his wife and son would be home in a short week from Europe, he had to understand that the remaining time could be as "lengthy" as he wanted, despite the fact that when they returned, his experiments would be drastically reduced—if not entirely curtailed.

The thought reminded him of the distractions he had to avoid; he had to keep a clear, open mental focus. "Forget everything but this present moment as you experience it," he told himself. He stared gently, gently, out the window. He watched the white lace curtain move softly in the night June air. He watched the moonlight blink and tremble on the back hitching post . . . and on the dark leaves of the lilac bushes, and . . .

George frowned and nervously twirled the edges of his fine moustache: everything was quiet, yet he *felt* things stirring beneath it all. He stared at the rolltop desk in the corner—or rather, he stared at where he knew it was; for it was mostly invisible in the darkness. His journal was in the desk drawer. He wanted to make some notations and yet he didn't want to move, lest he break the spell that he was trying to get himself into. It seemed that the soft air pulsated with urgency, as if there was something he was supposed to do. And he had no idea what it could be.

Patiently and stubbornly he tried another tactic, one that often worked. He'd largely given up sniffing laughing gas ever since he discovered that he could do things with his consciousness without it and control events better, besides. So now he tried to get out of his body using what he called Method One.

He lay down, relaxed himself completely, closed his eyes and felt around inside himself for what he called the invisible muscles of his astral body. Then, he tried to sit up—while his body lay still; to move inner arms while his physical ones lay crossed on his chest, to walk on astral legs while his physical ones lay flat against the bed.

"Uh, ug." He groaned with the effort. The sound was like thunder. His body shuddered. "Thunderation," he cried; realizing that he'd used too much effort, tried too hard. Now he'd have to start all over again! At the same time, he was growing sleepy. He yawned, annoyed with himself. Then another idea came to him. He'd use Method Five if he could remember it. He'd use his own sleepiness to advantage.

Usually George Brainbridge was all for the importance of will power, resolution and effort. He was learning, though, that sometimes these got in the way of his very special mental activities. So now, grudgingly, he gave in and tried a method of getting out of his body that took full advantage (or so it seemed to him) of the body's slavish need for sleep. He let his sleepiness come on. Trickily, he courted it. He yawned deeply, as if to tempt sleep to come closer. His eyes were closed; his bony body heavy on the cot's surface.

He let sleep come on, let sleep have its way. And this was the trick: at the same time he conjured up an image of himself in the hall outside his room. When he fell asleep—at that very precise moment—just before his consciousness "went under," he'd transfer it (and himself) to that other waking image.

His breathing was getting deeper. Was it time yet? His mind was getting . . . wavery; yet it was still . . . too alert; just a touch of wakefulness of the wrong kind. His breathing was even deeper— and deeper—he was *so* near sleep. Yet at the same time, craftily, he held the image of himself intact in his mind's eye. He mentally watched it. It was perfect: thinning brown hair, hawk-like nose, red dressing gown. He avoided getting sidetracked by details, though, and felt his consciousness gently begin a rolling motion that by now he'd learned to recognize. It was as if his consciousness were about to roll off a hill, into sleep's oblivion. And just when he got that feeling, George (Eureka! he shouted mentally) rolled his consciousness into the image, in which he was now fully awake. He congratulated himself and avoided the temptation to go back and look at his body because sometimes when he did, he just fell right back into it, so to speak, and that was that.

"Now then. What now?" he mused, listening and watching. Was everything as it should be? It was still night. He was still in the hall, so he went down to the second floor.

What a delicious secret triumph, to be walking around out of his body! George thought of indulging in his favorite sport—walking or flying around the block at night out of his body. The only thing that stopped him was that once he went through the front door, the outside environment frequently changed, and then he had to be very alert and in good shape to handle the situation. As he mused, he walked down the hall of the second floor and paused. The bedroom doors were closed. Suddenly he knew that he wasn't alone.

Cautiously, George Brainbridge walked through the first door into the western bedroom. The moon shone through the window, and George noted several things at once. The familiar bedroom furniture was gone. The gas lamps were gone from the walls, and lamps without wicks sat on the bedside tables.

Now what was going on? George wondered. Excited, he bent down to get a closer look. Wires running from the lamps led to an outlet of some kind in the baseboards; he had to be in the future. These must be future electric lights, amplifications of the simple models he'd read of in his journals. What a boon to dentistry!

He almost chortled. Yet at the same time, he knew that if he got too excited, he might lose control and be swept back to his body. Was this *his* house, in the future? Then who was sleeping in the bed that stood where his own should be? He bent closer. The moonlight shone on a man's face, and George Brainbridge stared; there was definitely a family resemblance. This man looked more like him than his own son did. Zounds! He bent closer.

Too late he noticed the wires leading from the light blanket. He touched the blanket gently—tiny shocks went through him, and the shocks were somehow translated into those weird crackling sounds that he found so curious. There must be electricity—in the *blanket?* In his consternation, George swore. But if he was out of his body, why should electricity bother him, if that *was* electricity? His consciousness started to stray. The scene began to get dim.

In desperation, George concentrated on the bedside table in front of his eyes, trying to keep it in focus. The smell of the late lilacs rushed up from the yard. The bedside table became increasingly visible. Then George heard a strange buzzing in his ears, or the sound of fire crackling, and suddenly a dizzying shift in his consciousness almost made him stagger. He felt as if he were flying through immense distances, even though he could plainly see that he hadn't moved an inch.

This time George's excitement nearly *did* sweep him back to his body, but his curiosity was even stronger; it kept him rooted to the spot, though for a moment his consciousness twanged like a rubber band, trying to be snapped in two places at once.

The room was the same, but again the furniture was different. Soft lights emerged from the ceiling, though George couldn't see their source. A group of people, looking as if they were on a tour, stood looking at the room in which he stood. There were ohs and ahs, but no one saw him. Was he hallucinating all this? George wondered. "Let all hallucinations vanish," he commanded mentally, with more confidence than he felt.

Nothing happened. George gasped; if he was right, then the people and room would have vanished if he were creating them himself. So he must have outdone himself. But where was he, and what was going on?

A voice came out of the walls, and George leapt back. "This is a replica of The George's bedroom, containing artifact copies found or reconstructed from the original tell. The exact age is uncertain, but certainly these furnishings were in vogue before the mid-1900's. You'll notice the ancient electric blanket, of course, plugged into wall sockets. Lamps that were turned off and on by hand."

This was the most vivid out-of-body experience George had ever had. He was jubilant. He tried to see and hear everything he could, for later notation in his journal. At the same time, the clarity of the affair frightened him, too. Everything was almost *too* clear. Suppose . . . he couldn't get back?

But before he could really worry about that, George noticed something else that shocked him to the core. The visitors, or whoever they were, men and women alike, wore short colorful tunics, with bare arms and legs everywhere flashing, and no one showed the slightest embarrassment. For a moment he wondered if he'd somehow traveled to some weird brothel. But no; the visitors obviously were staring at the room as if it were . . . a museum piece.

The invisible voice went on: "Who knows how many evenings The George spent back in those ancient times, experimenting with various states of consciousness until finally he came upon the Codicils? And without the Codicils, our world surely would not exist. Mankind's beliefs to that point were so self-destructive that only annihilation could have resulted."

"*The* GEORGE?" George felt dizzy again, and when he heard the word *Codicils*, more shocks went through his dream body. Every portion of his consciousness became super alert; the word seemed to fill his mind. CODICILS. . . .

More crackling sounds. Darkness, light. Then darkness. The next thing George knew, he snapped back to his body. Physically he was shouting, "The Codicils! The Codicils!" The sound of his own voice was so loud that it frightened him.

He looked around and checked the clock. It was 11 P.M. He was wide awake, and more excited than he could remember being in years. Quickly he put on his slippers, went out into the hall and down to the second floor. He opened the door to the western bedroom. Everything was the way it should be. His familiar bed sat there, empty. The gaslamps were in their accustomed places on the wall. He stroked his moustache and sighed. "Maybe the house is haunted," he thought.

George Brainbridge the Third was thinking exactly the same thing as his grandfather closed the door. George woke up with his scalp prickling. He shook his head, bemused; he could have sworn that someone was in the room for a minute. Shit. He sat up, turned off the electric blanket which was set at its lowest summer temperature because the old house got damp even on the warmest nights, put his pants on over his naked body, plunged his feet into his shoes, and headed for the kitchen. He'd never experienced a crazier week in his life, he thought. He wished Jean and the kids were back so that life could become commonplace again.

The light was on. George heard voices. Shit again, he thought. All he wanted was a sandwich and a moment's peace, and instead Seven must be talking to that damn Window, because now he heard voices clearly.

"What's going on down here?" he called, with joking peevishness, as he approached the kitchen door.

Chapter Fourteen

Dire Probability

"Hi," Seven said, brightly.

"Who's that with you? Window, Monarch, or Christ?" asked George, grinning.

"Verily. I'm Christ just now," Window said. "That's just super," George exclaimed brusquely. "All we need, I'd say." Then to Seven, "What the hell is really going on around here? Do you know? I'll be so glad to get back to my 'Tooth and Gums Business' tomorrow that I'm tempted to pay the patients."

Seven grinned sympathetically, but George said, "No kidding. I mean it. All this shit is driving me out of my mind. None of it *should* have happened—Christ healing Diggs; all those hallucinations or whatever they were at the restaurant; Window thinking he's two

97

people, Christ and some guy in the future. Tomorrow he goes back to the Center. That's that!"

"Are you Judas?" Christ asked, with mild curiosity.

"No, godammit," George replied. "I'm just a poor bemused tooth doctor."

"If they crucify me. . . ." Christ began.

"Will you stop that?" George interrupted, "They don't crucify people in this country anyhow. . . ."

"Bless you," Christ answered.

"Hell," George replied, "I like you better when you're Window."

At the same time, George's voice turned quizzical: When Window thought he was Christ—aside from the pat phrases about Judas and getting crucified—there *was* an aura about him. Suddenly George leaned forward and said dramatically, "You aren't *really* afraid of being crucified, are you? And you *know* I'm not Judas. What in the hell are you trying to pull? I'm mystified, I admit it."

"Well," demanded a voice, "are you going to tell him or not?"

George started with surprise as Gregory Diggs came in through the open back porch door. "What is this, a convention?" George said. "I suppose you couldn't sleep, either."

"I wasn't about to leave you guys alone with Mr. Window here," said Gregory, leering. Then to Seven, "Well?"

"Uh, it's sort of a wild story," Seven said, dubiously.

"Try me," George responded dryly. He sat down at the kitchen table, sighing with mock despair; then grinning. "Come on, guys. Give. This is an elaborate put-on."

This time Seven sighed. He put down his peanut butter sandwich, spread out his hands, and said, "This is it, the truth as we understand it after talking to Window-Christ-Monarch half the night. Ready?"

"Shoot," George said. He crossed his legs. "Nothing will surprise me," he added.

"Okay," Seven answered. "Window, interrupt me if I say anything you don't agree with. But it looks like this. That person" (he pointed to Window) "is the combination of the characteristics that belong to Window, Christ, and Monarch. Only for some reason, the characteristics are separate; he hasn't put them together. Now he *can* heal. We know that. He claims to come from the future or to see into it when he's Monarch."

"Yeah?" George said, with a silly unbelieving grin.

"I *am* Monarch," Window said suddenly and gently.

"Oh, Christ," George sputtered, before Seven shushed him.

At the same time, Diggs poked George and pointed to his own lap where a small cassette recorder was balanced on his knees. He turned it on to record.

Window-Monarch's face was grave. He said softly, "I'd like to believe that somehow or other I was speaking with George, *The* George, who initiated the Codicils into the world. Are you The George?"

George couldn't rid his face of its embarrassed perplexity. He wanted to say, "No, and I'm not Judas either!" But with some surprise he heard his voice respond differently: "Hell, I know about the Codicils," he said.

As he spoke, George heard Seven gasp. At the same time, Window's eyes certainly seemed to belong to someone else. They stared urgently at George. "I had the worst feeling that . . . something had happened in the past," Monarch said softly. "As if probabilities were changing. As if I had to contact you in your present time . . . I'll try again soon. I'm not as good at this as I should be—" As the words faded, Window's eyes lost the intentness. Himself again, he said, "That time I almost saw something . . . through someone else's eyes—"

But Seven was on his feet. "George, what do you know about the Codicils?" he asked. "Quickly."

"What is this?" asked George, bewildered. "When he said 'Codicils,' I just remembered seeing the word on the title page of one of my grandfather's old journals in the attic someplace. That's all—*The Codicils*. That was the title of one of his journals. He labelled them all; I don't even know if they're still up there."

And Seven cried, "They've got to be."

When Seven was with mortals, he had to act like them as much as possible so as not to give himself away. It was with considerable relief then that he rushed up to the attic, after getting George's permission to search for his grandfather's old journals. George, Window, and Diggs were off to bed in the second floor bedrooms.

Seven went into the attic, turned on the light, and closed the door behind him. The steady thumping of his heart distracted him ("All that racket," he cried), so he stepped out of his twentieth-century body after arranging it neatly on the old cot that stood by the window. He wondered if that cot was in another time occupied by another body—George the First's, for example?

Seven looked around. What he saw was the dirty, cluttered twentieth-century attic, with boxes stashed all over, antique furniture standing at odd angles, and the smell of dust mingling with the scent of lilacs that came in through the opened window. It was then that

Seven spied the old desk. It was the same one that had stood polished and gleaming in the attic study of George the First. Quickly Seven went rummaging through the drawers until finally he found what he was looking for. It was too much to ask for, he thought, grinning, as he came upon the neat stack of old journals.

Still, Seven paused before opening the one at hand. Was their author, George the First, invisibly there? And if he was, would *his* desk drawers open as if by an invisible hand? Or would his journals and desk drawers remain motionless? Because as Seven thought of opening the first journal, he felt very close to George the First—close enough to touch him, in fact.

Seven paused, staring. He studied the positions of the old journals, now scattered on the floor and looked at the dusty surface of the desk. Everything seemed complete twentieth-century except—Seven squinted his eyes—except for one tiny circle of air. Well, the circle wasn't tiny exactly, he thought, and he wasn't even sure how he knew it was different from all of the other air in the attic room, but it *was*.

Seven stared at the shiny segment of space suspiciously and hopefully at the same time. He simply had to discover what George the First knew about the Codicils! Was that odd super-transparent circle of space somehow connected with the same space in the 1890s? Because now Seven felt closer than ever to George the First—and more than that, he smelled a difference between that significant spot of air, and all the rest in the room.

Seven grinned: he had it! His inner senses were much more acute than the physical ones that came with his body, of course, and now he realized that the smell of dust and lilacs was everywhere else in the attic—*except* in that circle of space he was staring at. He stepped closer, thinking that here, for some reason, the times of both Georges must intersect.

In the next moment, though, Seven stepped back so quickly that he almost fell over, because suddenly a very real and solid red-sleeved lower arm and red-cuffed hand appeared in the center of the circle of space; it reached out and picked up the nearest journal that Seven hadn't yet placed with the others. And as the hand (surely George the First's) grabbed the journal, the dust instantly vanished from it; its color brightened, and the journal looked quite new.

"George? George?" Seven yelled—mentally, since he was out of his body. No one answered. Instead the hand flipped open the journal

100

and began to write with a fountain pen. "George, what do you know about the Codicils?" Seven cried, again getting no response.

At the same time almost, Seven gasped as he saw what was happening. The effect was somewhat like looking at a round television screen, whose stations automatically synchronized places and times. That is, the round circle in space shimmered. George's hand and the journal disappeared. There were wavy lines and warps in the circle, and then George's hand appeared again, only this time it was obvious that the hand was part of a statue—one of George that must stand in the twenty-fifth-century museum.

Seven's head was swimming. He concentrated as hard as he could on George in the 1890s, and after some more wavy lines, the circle in space changed. There was George's hand again, already having written several sentences in the open journal.

The picture stabilized. As quickly as he could, Seven began to read the sentences even as George's hand wrote on in neat script:

June 2, 1892

Tonight, having finally achieved an out-of-body condition, I first found myself in the western bedroom, only the time seemed to be somewhere in the future. I'm convinced that some electrical devices were in evidence, far superior to our current knowledge of that new field; though I wasn't quick enough to discover their workings. In a strange vision, I also saw a man sleeping in a bed where my bed should be. My intuitions told me that he was a future relative, and surely there was a family resemblance. This episode reminds me that a few days ago, in an altered state of consciousness while sniffing gas, I encountered a man who told me I had a grandson. Obviously I do not, and my son isn't married. Yet . . . Is it possible that I actually saw a future grandson sleeping in the room that is now my bedroom (when I use it)? When Sarah is away of course, I practically live in this attic hideaway except for handling my patients, very nicely I must admit, in the morning hours.

Seven frowned. That was as far as George got on the page, and his hand was now in the way. What about the Codicils? And where was Cyprus? It was obvious that she'd simplified his mission considerably. He was worried about everything.

George's hand moved down a few lines. Impatiently, Seven read:

101

The other adventure was equally mysterious, and I'm not sure how much hallucination was involved. I found myself again, it seemed, in the western bedroom in some distant future, only the room was a museum piece. The furniture was an odd mixture of what is now in my bedroom, and the furniture that I saw in it in the previous instance. People who certainly seemed alive were staring at the room. They were dressed in the flimsiest of apparel, and though I'm far from being narrowly moralistic, I was somewhat shocked, and at first thought I might be in a brothel.

George's hand was in the way again, and Seven almost cried with impatience. If *he* saw George's hand, did George sense that someone was watching *him?* Could he, Seven, reach into that magic space and pull the journal back? Seven grinned, imagining George's startled reaction (He'd probably scream, "Zounds."). And anyway, what good would that do? Seven wondered. None. So he waited.

George's hand was trembling. He began to write in a faster, agitated manner.

Now we come to the heart of the matter. A man's voice came out of the walls in some way unknown to me, but surely some future development of the gramophone was involved. The voice spoke about "the Codicils" with a significance of tone that gave the phrase "the Codicils" great import. Something was said, if I remember correctly, about "The George" or "in the time of George," or words to that effect. But the impact of those words upon myself was unprecedented. I felt them to the core of my soul. The entire affair may be symbolic rather than literal, of course, and I've had enough experience with states of consciousness to know how insidious hallucinations can be—if you accept them as real. But ever since [and here, the handwriting became very agitated] *I began my adventures in consciousness, I felt that there was a reason for them. And tonight I* knew *that I have to discover The Codicils, whatever they are.*

My only clue is in the distant future just mentioned. And I have no assurance that I can return there. I tried several out-of-body methods before achieving success last time. Did the last one I used somehow propel me into other times as well? Of course I'll experiment further, for even as I write, a sense of urgency that I do not understand overtakes me. And in a week my wife and son will return from Europe, in which case my opportunities for experimentation will be drastically reduced.

And, Seven thought, in a week Jean and the kids would return to George the Third. . . .

Seven couldn't believe what he was reading. George hadn't discovered the Codicils yet! And Seven had hoped to learn them from George, to give to Window in the twentieth century. With dismay, Seven stared again at the journal page. The circle in space barely contained it, and again George's hand was in the way. But again Seven managed to glimpse the date at the top of the page—*June 2, 1892*—and he shook his head in confusion. It was June 2, 1982, in the attic, and in the world of George, Josephine, Gregory, and Window. Then apparently George the First had had his out-of-body encounters while Window and Diggs sat with Seven in the kitchen just a short "time" ago; and before George got out of bed to see what was going on.

These thoughts came and went, but since Seven realized that George hadn't discovered the Codicils, a sense of foreboding began to assail him. At first his dismay merely grew sharper. Then, however, the circle of space in which the journal appeared began to darken, shimmer, and tremble until finally it seemed to whirl into darkness altogether. It became a black circle of space darker than the space about it and somehow threatening. If the Codicils weren't discovered 'in time' Seven wondered, what probable worlds might vanish? Could they actually disappear? And how could the Codicils appear in the twenty-fifth century and form the basis of a world, if they hadn't *already* been planted in the past? Seven looked around anxiously. The black circle was . . . expanding, while at the same time it grew even blacker, and more concentrated. And compelling.

Seven thought he heard Cyprus cry, "Seven, look away. Quick." But it was too late. Events began to happen and unhappen with such rapidity that Seven instinctively knew he was in trouble. In a flash he dismissed his own mental image of himself, so that he was invisible consciousness. (And just in time, as he said to Cyprus later, "Because that circle or hole or whatever was like a multidimensional meat-grinder; any kind of form at all would be . . . well, ground up.")

His consciousness actually twirled topsy-turvy, turned inside out, sideways . . . if consciousness had a shape, it was pulled out of it, so that Seven first felt long, then short, then big, then small, then absolutely "not there." The circle that had opened up through the universe itself, it seemed, was like an eternally ravenous animal-of-space. Seven felt as if he was falling down some infinite tunnel. Even that idea didn't fit, though, because Seven felt that time was so scrambled that while he was falling through the tunnel on the one hand, on the other hand, another part of him was poised eternally on its threshold—staring, unable to move. And that part didn't know about this tumbling-through-the-tunnel-self at all.

And worse: As fast as these events kept happening, they kept unhappening at the same time, so that yet another part of him felt as if he was tumbling back the other way through the hole he'd just entered. Not only that, but somewhere along the way, space had vanished; that is, it felt as if space knotted up into itself . . . or he himself was knotting up into space, so that even his thoughts had no psychological room between them but kept bumping into one another, *sticking* to each other like glue until there was just one clump of thoughts like porcupine quills—and then *that* vanished.

Psychological silence.

Seven knew he was thinking at an incredibly fast rate—but somehow no thoughts registered. He was himself, and he felt oddly cool and quiet, though he had nothing to judge himself against. He existed . . . in reference to nothing. So how did he know he existed? He thought the question, but it didn't register, and all Seven knew was that . . . his thinking seemed to exist apart from himself, with no connection to himself. And "at the same time" in this silence he felt that unendurable energy surrounded him, making energy-falls instead of say, waterfalls; and that this energy felt solid even though its motion blurred the edges of his consciousness.

This particular experience seemed endless. He kept falling through this chute with the moving walls of energy; yet knowing this, he didn't feel as if he were falling. Or rather, he felt suspended, unmoving *and* moving at once. Even the darkness around him moved, varied in intensity, trembled, formed shapes of darkness within darkness.

Seven was beyond fear. He even began to feel a part of whatever strange process was occurring, as if he and the process were one.

His thoughts had felt compressed and inaccessible to him. Now they began to gyrate within his consciousness; to swirl. Simultaneously, he felt a fantastic pull from some distance "in front of him" and suddenly he *did* feel as if he was falling. And falling fast. In the next "moment" Seven saw a rim of light so bright that he thought physical eyes could never stand it. And before he could even begin to wonder about this, there was a light, floating sensation, an odd popping sound—and Seven found himself standing in what he knew at once was another universe altogether.

Seven gulped, figuratively speaking. He was definitely in another universe or *un*universe, he thought, for he sensed negation everywhere. The atmosphere was peculiarly suffocating; the air heavy and motionless. Yet the environment was physical enough. There were ugly dwarf bushes everywhere; miles of greyish sand, and the sky was a threatening purple-grey, with fog reaching from a few feet above the ground, hanging almost motionless for what seemed to be miles, at least, before the thick levels of purple-grey sky began.

It was difficult to say whether it was night or day; the place seemed to exist in an eternal twilight. The mountains in the distance were devoid of growth, their naked rock and dirt ledges looking like eerie steps to nowhere. The longer Seven stood where he was, the more aware he became of the heavy atmosphere. Even though he was without a body, he felt as if he weighed tons. Or—no, he felt as if his *thoughts* weighed tons; as if his very psychological being was too heavy a burden to bear.

Anxious, he looked more closely around him. He was on some kind of ancient fortification, on the second or third floor, for above him now he saw half-destroyed floors; and he was standing only on a fairly small ledge, obviously all that was left of this part of the fortress. It was made of wood; much of it now rotten and as Seven squinted in the distance he realized that the ruins of hundreds of such structures lay in piles and heaps on the grey ground, blending in so well with this weathered world, that he hadn't distinguished them as structures at all.

A glint of metal at Seven's feet caught his eye. He squinted down at it sideways. It was a broken-off metal plaque. Seven read the weathered lettering: "Skirmish 541. World War V."

World War Five? The implications made Seven dizzy. The structures or their remains *were* fortresses, then. When he thought *that*, Seven's inner senses showed him a sudden scene: thousands of men and women, living and fighting in this area thousands of years ago, building and rebuilding the fortresses; literally a decayed species, dying of—

Of despair. The emotion was so strong that Seven cried out, as he realized what this world, this universe was. Created by man's despair, it was a future probable universe in which man answered none of the questions that plagued him in George's time.

Seven looked up again; there were no floating cities in that sky, either, no evidence of man's technology or adventuresomeness. In *this* reality, the species didn't last that long. It was then that Seven noticed the silence. Not one bird call or insect sound. No murmuring of the wind. He looked down: no anthills. It was a final version of the dire visions he'd seen earlier.

And Seven knew that no one could withstand that atmosphere of despair. It caught at his own consciousness; he felt his own thoughts darkening. Desolation stained even his inner vision until he feared that his spiritual sight would be forever dimmed by a cast of darkness. Was this what mortals felt, when they experienced despair? Did George feel that way? Or Window? Or Diggs or Josephine? As if nothing mattered and no meaning existed? They never *said* that to themselves or to each other, Seven thought, confused. And Monarch?

And the instant Seven thought of Monarch, he remembered *the* Codicils. This he realized was a universe in which the Codicils didn't exist and were never discovered; in which they remained psychologically invisible to man. But what about Christianity? Seven wondered, even as he struggled against the growing closeness of the air. *What about Christianity?*

Suddenly, brightly, in his mind's eye Seven saw Window speaking as Christ as he had done in George's kitchen earlier, and then speaking for Monarch. And as he saw this inner vision, Seven cried out. For Window . . . *was* himself Window and yet a personification of the people of George's time. Christianity as it had been known was dead-ended. The twentieth-century world still wasn't big enough to accept miracles as fact; and so Christ became a delusion. And man had to take the steps that would lead him beyond what he was—to become . . . Monarch. Man had to find the Codicils.

Seven felt more helpless and forlorn than he ever remembered being. How could one soul, even a Seven, discover such a vital message—when he didn't even know what the Codicils said exactly, or how to find them? And if he didn't, did it mean that *this* terrible world would be the future of George's Earth? The sense of responsibility felt crushing, yet Seven told himself that he'd accept it—if he had to; if there was no other way, if. . . .

"I'll find the Codicils," he shouted; and as he did, he gasped in astonishment. He'd felt the air get closer, but now it had collected tightly around him so that it formed a circle filled, it seemed, with new magnetic darkness. And before he could understand what was happening, he began to fall once more through the tunnelling dimensions from which he'd only shortly emerged.

Space turned into time, time into space. Seven's thoughts suddenly had incredible mass—and then seemed to disappear altogether. In between, he told himself that he didn't care what happened; he'd find the Codicils. Only once, when his thoughts appeared clearly, did he wonder nostalgically where George's world was now; and the attic room where his body still lay neatly on the twentieth-century couch.

Did George's world even exist?

Was it there, to return to?

Chapter Fifteen

Cyprus Introduces Seven to Framework Two, and George I Visits the Museum of Time

---

"Of course George's world exists," Cyprus said.

As he heard Cyprus' words, Seven felt as if he were being pulled (by the hair of his head) out through the other end of the mysterious chute in which he'd found himself. Once again, times and places came together and made sense, just as his thoughts once more came in clear sentences.

"You just haven't learned the grammar of energy yet," Cyprus said. Seven heard her, but he couldn't yet sense her presence.

"Grammar of energy!" Seven cried, mentally. "That experience was awful."

"You just got caught in the middle of a process, the process by which energy speaks its atomic structure," Cyprus' voice answered.

"But where are you?" Seven asked quarrelsomely. "And where am I? I just feel suspended. . . ." Seven broke off, for suddenly he felt . . . portions of himself coming together and joining him, like thousands of glowing bolts of energy hopscotching to join his own consciousness. "Oh," he said, in a small voice. "Oh. Now I remember."

"Well, remember more, and you'll be in Framework Two with me," Cyprus replied.

"Remember what?" Seven thought, but even as he asked the question, the returning bolts of energy joined with his consciousness so quickly that he forgot the question. He didn't need it any longer. As the energy mixed and merged with his own awareness, Seven cried, "Of course," and instantly a group of images appeared. At the same time, Seven saw Cyprus waiting for him—and he gasped as Framework Two formed about him.

They were standing in a natural garden in which each flower seemed to be the most beautiful one that Seven had *ever* seen in any space or time. Each leaf also seemed to be itself, and more than a leaf at the same time. Surrounding the garden grew the liveliest forest that Seven could imagine; each tree more supple and delightful than any Seven had ever seen. He could hardly begin to examine the environment. Even the air had the sweetest odor, as if it were the essence from which all summer air was distilled.

Cyprus said, "Seven, because you're an earth soul, I thought you'd like Framework Two to look like this," and Seven was so enchanted that he could hardly answer. At the same time, the landscape was constantly changing as if a million summers were forming.

Cyprus had also outdone herself as far as her image was concerned, but exactly *what* she'd done was almost impossible for Seven to discover. It wasn't just that she looked like the model from which all female and male elements were first drawn—being at the same time handsome and beautiful, athletic and supple, combining all of the characteristics of each sex in one form—but that these characteristics seemed intensified to an incredible degree. . . .

"You're on the right track," Cyprus said.

"But . . . everything looks . . . brand-new," Seven cried. "As if it were all created this instant. I mean, that one rose—look, there, the third one in from the first row. It's a bud, so of *course* it looks new. But beside it is a much bigger rose, with all of its petals opened, and *it* looks brand-new too!"

"Precisely," Cyprus replied, with the most innocent and yet the most enigmatic smile.

"And the older trees look as fresh or . . . new, anyhow, as the younger ones," continued Seven, even more puzzled.

"Exactly," Cyprus said, smiling more mysteriously than ever. "You almost have it."

With that Seven shouted, "And you're always magnificent when you want to be. But now, now you're so much . . . *more* like yourself . . . that you're almost like a Model for yourself—" Seven's thoughts swirled. His intuitions made connections that left him breathless. He cried, "You *are*. . . the source from which the usual you emerges!"

And Cyprus said very gently, "And here, Seven, so are you." As she spoke, Seven realized that her words were literally true. He felt himself . . . growing out of his own larger source, and at the same time, he was the source from which he was ever emerging.

In that instant, Oversoul Seven felt himself turn into pure aware-ized energy—his identity stamping itself upon the universe; energy turning into who he was, in a process unending. His awareness was vast, yet with each detail sharp and clear as if it alone existed. And within his awareness, Seven saw George the First and George the Third, and Window who was also Monarch in the twenty-fifth cen-tury.

"They're separate! Inviolately themselves, each like no one or any-thing else in the universe," Seven called out in exaltation to Cyprus. "But . . . they're counterparts of each other, too."

"There's more," said Cyprus' voice, and it turned into waves of energy, flowing all about them. The waves turned into sparkling im-ages. Seven gasped, figuratively speaking, for there before him stood both of the Georges, and Window, and Monarch . . . and—he gasped—Josephine and Gregory Diggs. Only these mortals—all his personalities, he realized—were more than mortals, as the roses and trees were more than roses and trees. They were multidimensional models of themselves, brilliant with infinite potentials and abilities; they were personal psychological banks sources from which they drew the personified energy of the universe.

As this was happening, Seven's own consciousness took form after sparkling mental form. *He* was Window and Josephine and Diggs. *His* energy automatically, splendidly, and spontaneously formed their lives. Even now he felt a portion of himself nestled in a cell in the crook of Gregory Diggs's arm as Gregory slept in the twentieth-cen-tury world—

"And more," Cyprus said. And Oversoul Seven felt his identity swept up into a new, different vastness—he was couched in a clear psychological universe in which he was everywhere supported. His memory instantly refreshed itself; of course, he thought, without thinking in our terms at all. Now he remembered his own birth—and his constant rebirth—in this inner indescribable universe that automatically formed itself into individuation, Framework Two. And he felt himself intact, with more powers and potentials and desires and purposes than he knew he had, and Seven knew that he was within the mental reality that was Cyprus's.

He didn't think he could comprehend anything beyond this, but even as he thought *that*, Cyprus's reality opened up and he sensed even more magnificence of which she herself was but a part. Yet in all of this, his identity rode securely, jubilantly, safely—boldly and exuberantly. He felt as if he was the youngest being in the universe, and that he was being shown the model for his own future growth.

"But there's more," Cyprus said. "Watch closely." And for a moment, everything vanished except for a small earthen hut on a hillside that suddenly sprang out of nowhere. Almost instantly, on the same spot, a million other buildings seemed to be transposed over the hut, and its environment steadily expanded. Seven counted at least a hundred cities, each one beginning from the hut or springing out of it; and then, from each sparkling building he saw, another new structure sprang into being. There were too many styles and cultures to count. He saw Byzantine palaces and their boulevards; the twenty-fifth-century floating cities, splendid European and Indian castles, temples, and Medieval villages as well as Arabian bazaars. And in each case, these separate civilizations remained themselves, while in each of them, all of the others were somehow implied.

"The models for every possible civilization exist here," Cyprus said. "And each possible eccentric variation is given freedom."

"The Codicils," Seven shouted. "They have to be models for civilization—"

Smiling, Cyprus answered, "Exactly."

"Well, then, I've got to find them," Seven cried. "And at once."

"Shush," Cyprus said. "I'll make this easy for you by cutting out anything that doesn't apply to the problem. Look."

And Seven saw George the First in his attic study, trying another "out-of-body." The picture was clear and detailed, fully sensed, so that Seven even smelled the lilacs out in George's back yard.

George was out-of-body. He kept muttering, "I've got to find the Codicils, whatever they are, before it's too late." His dream body wore a mental version of his favorite red dressing gown. He half-

111

walked and half-floated down the hallway, thinking, "I've got to get to the future where I saw the museum."

And as George thought *that*, Seven held his breath in surprise (figuratively speaking), because George disappeared from the 1890's picture and suddenly appeared in an adjacent twenty-fifth-century one. *There* he stood in front of the museum.

"I admit I'm startled," Seven said. "But from here, it's so easy to see how it's done. I didn't have to worry about juggling time, or going through space atom by atom so to speak; you just . . . state your intent—"

"And in Framework Two, you can move through any time period that exists in Framework One, which is all the earthly dimensions," Cyprus added.

George shook his dream head with happy puzzlement. "Now how did I do that?" he wondered. "And—zounds—what do I do next?"

Seven grinned; there was the museum—the twenty-fifth-century version of George's house. And to Seven, the walls suddenly became transparent. In an upper room, supposed to be a replica of George's study, a statue stood staring out the window. Seven saw all the rooms, each more or less bearing a resemblance to the twentieth-century ones he knew. But he noticed something else—a lower room, in the cellar. As soon as he wanted to examine the details, the picture zoomed in closer. A gold plaque read, "Ye old bomb shelter." And just inside there were some glass cases. Seven peered closer. The sign read: "Replica of the Codicil microfilm, discovered in the tell of 2550."

Seven started to cry, "Microfilm?" when he noticed another larger plaque, filled with writing and headed: "The Codicils." "There they are," he shouted to Cyprus. "All I have to do is—"

Cyprus shook her head. "You can't do it *for* George. He has to find them himself . . . and sift their message back to his own version of them."

Now what does *that* mean? Seven wondered, but mentally he yelled out to George: "Go down to the basement."

George pulled his dressing robe tighter about him. "I think I'll go downstairs first, if I ever get inside," he thought. But his consciousness was wavering. He thought of his body with a touch of fear: had he been away from it too long? No—resolutely, he told himself that everything was all right. "It's all *all right*," he muttered for the tenth time, but something told him that it wasn't all right at all.

George realized that he had a headache—out of his body. How was that possible? he wondered. He started to float through the muse-

112

um's front door. At the same time, he became aware of a white light, seemingly in his head. The light frightened him, and as this happened, his consciousness flashed back to his body.

But damnation! George thought. It had taken him forever to get in decent out-of-body condition; he couldn't—wouldn't—miss the opportunity! He had to find the Codicils! Even his sense of urgency didn't surprise him. Since he'd first heard the words, they'd obsessed him. He concentrated as hard as he could.

Now he stood inside the museum. "Go downstairs," he told himself; wavering. The light came again, this time much more intense than before—and his inner mental space seemed to . . . expand in the oddest, quite frightening fashion, and the headache returned with double strength. Such a thing had never happened to him before.

He drifted downward; stairs were beneath him. He gritted his dream teeth—if he could just make it further . . . After all, what could happen? At the worst, he'd just plunge back into his body. Wouldn't he? Or had he really been gone too long?

Oversoul Seven was mentally yelling, "Go back to your body," but George never heard him, lost as he was in his resolute determination to reach the Codicils. "He *has* been out too long," Seven said to Cyprus. "Why doesn't he take the warning?"

"Because he's stubborn, like someone else I know," Cyprus said.

George saw a plaque. The light became almost blinding. For a moment, he was afraid that he could somehow disappear in its sensed vastness. His consciousness felt as if it were being pulled back to his body at an incredible rate. He looked down . . . his dream body gyrated over his physical one, then he blanked out for a moment, and blinking, sat up.

Cyprus and Seven turned into two bits of light on George's brass gaslamp.

"Well, he's all right now," Seven said. "But *I'm* not stubborn, if that's what you mean."

George sat up and lit his pipe.

"We'll discuss that later," Cyprus said. "Right now, I want to be sure that you understand what you have to do about the Codicils."

"Right-o," said Seven, grinning. "At least I think I do. Somehow even though George failed this time, I have to help him get the Codicils in the twenty-fifth-century museum and bring them back to the 1890's—"

"He can't bring back the plaque," Cyprus interrupted. "That object can't exist in George's time, but the ideas *can*. . . ."

"You mean, he has to memorize them?" Seven cried.

"Not necessarily."

"But he'll *never* memorize all the stuff I saw on that plaque," Seven protested. "He's bound to forget some things and distort others, and—"

"He'll be translating them into his own time scheme," Cyprus said gently. "After that, though, the Codicils have to be discovered in the time of George's grandson."

George put out his pipe, lay down, promptly fell asleep, and started snoring.

"But how?" Seven cried. "I'm really confused now. And if I don't get it all right, that awful probable Earth will come into being in George's world's future." He sighed. "Cyprus, you've given me too much to handle this time."

"Nonsense," Cyprus answered, looking nowhere in particular. "You can always do more than you think you can. You know about Framework Two now. It's really quite simple. George has to find the Codicils in the twenty-fifth-century museum, and write them down in his journal in the 1890s so that his grandson can find them in the attic in the twentieth century and put them on microfilm in the bomb shelter. *Then* they can be found by Monarch in the twenty-fifth century, as they *are* in that probable future. Nothing could be simpler!"

"But if I can't, what happens then? And it sounds impossibly complicated to me," Seven cried. He took on his fourteen-year-old male image to emphasize his lack of experience in such matters, and stood there, looking dismayed and put-upon. "And what about John Window and Josephine Blithe and Gregory Diggs and their problems?" he said glumly. "What do they have to do with all this?"

Cyprus took on her favorite image of the woman teacher, her face changing from an ancient, knowing one to a young one that nevertheless shone with the wisdom of age. She smiled and said softly, "Seven, I'm not going to give you *all* of the answers. And if I were you, I'd get busy. You left your body in the twentieth-century attic for one thing, and for another, probabilities are really spinning at this moment because George the Third is about to open up this attic door. So you'd better get back to the right time in a hurry."

"Now I'm so confused that I don't know how to," Seven protested. "I certainly don't want to go through that tunnel again either, if I don't have to."

Cyprus sighed. "Think of Framework Two," she directed. "It's

114

the Inside of every time and place. Concentrate on the time you want, and you'll come out there."

"You're sure?" Seven asked, dubiously. "And why didn't you tell me about Framework Two before?"

"I can't explain right now, but yes, I'm sure about the directions I just gave you. They won't work, though, unless you're sure, too."

"I'm sure," Seven said promptly. He imagined Framework Two as being the Insideness of all times and places, and then said mentally, "I want this room and time of night, but on June 2, 1982."

To help himself concentrate, he'd closed his mental eyes and when nothing seemed to be happening, he opened them. It worked! There was his nifty twentieth-century body, lying empty on the old cot. Seven grinned, and dived into the physical form—just in time.

The attic door opened, and George Brainbridge the Third stuck his head inside the room and bellowed, "Well, it's dawn. Did you find the damned journals?"

Chapter Sixteen

Brothers of the Mind, a Dream Investigation, and Paranoia from the Past

---

The Codicils were such a part of Monarch's mental life, and so self-explanatory, that it was extremely difficult for him to imagine what the world must have been like without them. He knew that the historians had left huge gaps in their story of man's progress. At the same time, as he prepared for the 500th anniversary, the cinquecentennial celebration of the Codicils' origin, Monarch found himself considering the pre-Codicil world with feelings of strong disquiet.

He'd been thinking how spectacular The George's achievement truly was, considering the background of his times; the fact that few if any people then embarked in any serious mental travel, and the fact that all of The George's previous training and belief systems must have been directly contrary to his own intuitive discoveries.

And, as always, standing in the museum's front hallway, Monarch felt the familiar thrilling sensations that indicated he was picking up information through an alternate neurological sequence. He could almost sense the presence of The George; still learning the inner mechanics of mental locomotion, wandering in a world none of his compatriots could find, until finally he came upon the Codicils. But how? That question had never been answered. It was a vital question, Monarch mused, because if the Codicils hadn't appeared in that ancient past, then surely he, Monarch, and all of the earth people, would have known an entirely different world. *If* mankind had even been able to survive at all without the Codicils, which didn't seem too likely.

Monarch shivered suddenly. The museum seemed almost eerie in the silence. Waiting. The workers had all left, after cleaning the place from top to bottom, touching up, washing the windows. Fresh flowers stood in vases on all of the tables. Only now, the vacuum cleaner turned itself off after soundlessly going over all of the floors. The place was supposed to represent The George's twentieth-century house—its ancient domestic arrangements, its stationary windows instead of moving window-walls, its boxed-in yet cozy interior. Monarch noted the fresh flowers, native species that, had perhaps once grown in The George's back yard.

Yet there was no doubt about it, Monarch thought uneasily, the flowers themselves had a different air than the house itself; they seemed . . . strangely modern. It was almost as if faded flowers would be more appropriate. Monarch smiled to himself, and at the same time he felt a stronger surge of . . . alienness enter the immaculate hall in which he stood.

His prominent narrow nose wiggled. He shivered again with mild surprise. "Is there anyone here?" he asked mentally.

At the same time he felt around inside his own consciousness for any patterns of sensation, however faint; for any information that seemed to be coming through those neural passageways with which he did not usually identify his consciousness. Faint whisperings. Strange—for he began to hear words, which then mentally appeared as letters that took the shape of a man. So! Monarch speculated: A man with that shape must be *speaking* the words.

A window frame appeared transposed over the man's figure. All of this was very faint, and even with the training given everyone throughout life, Monarch had trouble holding the images intact long enough to study them. Why the unaccustomed difficulty? he won-

117

dered. He closed his eyes to see the images better, then sighed as he interpreted the message: A man called Window was speaking. But to whom? About what? And how did the event have any connection with himself?

But there was . . . something! Monarch suddenly felt weak and leaned against the hallway table. The channel that had opened had a different feel to it . . . a vacant quality, as if some important ingredient were lacking. A message from a dank world—and Monarch's head suddenly snapped up—a world *before* the Codicils; a world seeking for them; and a personality living in that world . . . who was . . . another aspect of himself!

There was no doubt of it. Monarch knew the feel of his own essence. And if the Codicils had taught man anything, it was the multidimensionality of the self, which was seeded throughout the centuries. And he recognized that peculiar yet definite *alter-essence* that represented his own psychological acknowledgement of "another self." A self, Monarch thought, that would always be "other" to him as he would be "other" to it. Yet they were connected through neurological pathways that appeared ghostily, roaming through the worlds of their individual thoughts.

But why in a world prior to the Codicils?

What was that ancient self trying to tell him? Monarch broke off, correcting himself: That self existed simultaneously with his own life—the twentieth and twenty-fifth centuries coexisted.

"Brother of my mind, speak," Window said mentally.

No answer; only a steadily growing sense of anxiety. But about what? This time Monarch heard the words, "the Codicils," repeated several times, in a warning or at least highly anxious mental voice that now he accepted as his own. Were they about to be stolen? The Codicils themselves *couldn't* be stolen, Monarch thought; they were in the people's minds. The precious ancient microfilms could, but why? Monarch frowned again. It couldn't be that. He must be wrong.

Still pondering and uneasy, he walked up the front stairs, taking some comfort in his own muscular activity, automatically checking to see if everything was in readiness. How perfect it a'l looked; The George's house—preserved, as if he might return to it at any time. *At any time!* In another frame of reference, The George *was* here, Monarch thought suddenly. The idea had come to him many times before, but as a pleasant theoretical fantasy. It now occurred to him that fantasy or no, according to the principles laid down by the Codicils themselves, The George lived in this house or its facsimilie in the twentieth century even as he, Monarch, climbed the steps in the twenty-fifth. Then, what was The George doing now? And who was worried about the Codicils, and why? Surely they were safe enough, but what would anyone possibly gain by stealing them? The people would lose a vital artifact, a beloved symbol. . . .

Astonished with himself, Monarch broke off his line of thought and, almost dazed, reached the top of the stairs. His thoughts had actually been paranoid! He'd actually, seriously, been considering the possibility that someone would really steal the Codicils—and in a world where such social diseases had been completely eliminated for over a century! Whatever possessed him? To his knowledge, not one act of thievery had been committed in his lifetime; the causes had been eradicated almost naturally, as the Codicils taught man about his own potentials and abilities. The resentments and hatreds that had caused individual crimes no longer existed in the same way. Not that men were saints, but they were at least acting like members of a dignified species. They respected themselves and others.

Then how could he have seriously considered the possibility that the Codicils would be stolen, and felt such an intense anxiety? Of course, Monarch thought: The ideas hadn't been his own. When would he really learn to recognize the messages that rose up through his own familiar consciousness? That paranoia wasn't of his own time. Perplexed, Monarch sat down on the Victorian period chair at the top of the stairs. He knew that there were psychic correlations between himself and his "other" selves—invisible psychological intersections. And that fear about the Codicils had come from just such a channel. But why had he picked up that particular message now, just before the celebration of the finding of the microfilm at the dig? In two hours, the entire area would be mobbed with visitors from all over the world.

In two hours, the Codicils would be on view, of course.

The Holograph Players would perform the ceremonial drama—the history of the finding of the Codicils—and depict the life of The George.

Monarch sighed and decided to check with his mate, Leona, to see if her latest dream work had yielded any results that might throw light on this odd anxiety of his. He and Leona were both dream archeologists. But Leona had always been the best dreamer, Monarch thought. Sometimes at the last minute, she *had* come up with excellent dream data, as if a crisis stimulated her abilities. He frowned. His abilities didn't work that way; he liked peace and quiet. But there wouldn't be any until the celebration was over . . . and as he walked down the museum's hall, Monarch tried to throw aside the sudden nagging thought that the celebration itself was somehow threatened.

He opened the door to The George's bedroom; Leona spent her dreaming time there, in the hopes that the location might stimulate new information. She was looking out the windows and turned, almost anxiously, as Monarch entered.

"I'm done," she said, "and the room is in order—"

"But?" Monarch asked. He knew her so well that her anxiety was apparent, even as she tried to soften its expression by a reassuring smile.

"Well, I may have received some new facts . . . disturbing ones. Or at least, I may have some information that contradicts other things we think we know. I hate it when that happens." Her large brown eyes still carried hints of their dream visions. She seemed bathed in the softness of an alternate consciousness; not blurred, but carrying the look a child does when roused from sleep. Even her anxiety was softened by this aura of subjective refreshment. "The dreams are already recorded," she said. "I taped them at once." Her toes wiggled in her sandals; she tapped her right foot gently so that her ankle bracelets tinkled, and her short skirt rippled with the graceful motion. "Just think. These windows opened once. Or the originals did." Again she stared out at the museum's grounds.

"And let in all the dirt of traffic," Monarch said, laughing despite himself. It was a game they usually loved to play. They'd stand there, using their inner senses, trying to bring up to awareness's threshold all of the sounds of the ancient automobiles, the squeal of tires. . . . "Don't put me off, though. You're the best dreamer of the two of us. What did you come up with?"

She swung around. "*I* am? And whose dreaming led to this dig and resulted in the museum to begin with? Yours!"

"True," Monarch said. "But I've always felt that something was incomplete. . . ."

"Maybe it was," Leona said seriously. "You can check my dream records later. But there were *three* separate, clear dreams. In one, I stood in an ancient kitchen, much like the museum's, and there was a man named Window who was trying to look into our world."

Monarch's face almost drained of color.

"What's wrong?" asked Leona, alarmed.

"Go on," responded Monarch, "I'll tell you when you're through."

"Well," she said doubtfully, "I'll tell you the second one in sequence, though it's somewhat complicated. This dream was almost like a night-mare. In a terribly vivid series of events I saw . . . what the world would be like now if we didn't have the Codicils. It really was some-what frightening, but I kept my head and my critical functions throughout. . . ." She paused, then continued quickly. "Some—most—of the ideas were sheer insanity. It was hard to understand, but in the dream, wars were considered a method of achieving peace. I mean, countries had armies, and the greater the war machines, the greater the chances of peace were considered to be! Idiocy, I told you. And in the dream, mankind hadn't learned how to handle tech-nology at all. Somehow it was used to build up a country's arsenal of possible retaliatory equipment." Leona shook her head almost an-grily. "The entire affair was most distasteful, and I was really amazed to find myself encountering such nonsense so directly. There was more," she went on, "but the third dream was the one I thought most significant."

Monarch nodded, knowing that they'd checked dream details and crosschecked them a thousand times in their ten years of keeping records.

"Well, in the third dream I was a woman, connected with the man Window, of the first dream. And my name was Josephine." Leona paused, then spelled out the name meaningfully.

Monarch stared at her. "You're saying that there's been an error in the legends? That the man we have as The George's closest friend was a woman?"

Leona answered slowly, "Not 'Joseph Ine' at all. But *Josephine*, a woman. I'm really quite sure . . . though where the man Window, fits in, I don't know."

"I can tell you that," Monarch replied. From a brief experience I had on the way up here, I think that Window was—is—one of my own aspects in the twentieth century."

"And if Josephine *was* an aspect of me, if I'm right—"

"Then somehow both of us were involved with The George. In some capacity at least," Monarch said. And more slowly: "That could be why I picked up the location of this dig to begin with."

Leona looked forlorn. "Then why have you had these dreadful feelings lately about the Codicils being in danger?"

Monarch sighed. "I don't know. The entire museum, the environ-ment, the grounds and the river sometimes lately seem . . . transitory, as if they could vanish in a moment."

"Then we have to conduct a Together Dream!" Leona cried.

"There's nothing else to do. We'll be our own dreamguides, we'll sleep in this bed . . . and try to dreamtravel into the past clearly—"

"There's so many variables," Monarch said. "I don't do my best dreamtravel under pressure, either, like you do . . . and there's not much time before the celebration, either. The technicians must be gathering in the basement and downstairs rooms even now."

She grinned at him.

He started laughing. "Of course you're right. And who knows what we'll find? Maybe we'll even have more new data for the celebration."

They took off all of their clothes and lay down in the replica of The George's bed. They let their thoughts melt: then they let their thoughts melt *together*, and they felt their bodies dissolving into the bedding—becoming the bedding as far as sensation was concerned, though both of their physical forms lay there, cool and quiet as sleeping stones. Their minds met where their thoughts merged together, and their dream-selves rose up like forms of smoke. The forms faded together into the room's past—into the pasts of the room—disappearing in numberless autumns and summers, floating through immeasurable winters and springtime . . . following the beckoning focuses of their individual and joint intents.

Monarch and Leona were naturally gifted dreamtravelers, their abilities tuned and developed through their university training. They loved working together, and now they maintained their separate critical consciousnesses carefully, clearly, easily, letting them ride atop the deeper, steadier dream consciousnesses that supported them. Their love for each other was a further support, adding to their closeness, so that now the dream consciousness of one of them could intermingle with the other's. But always their intent steered them in one direction: toward The George's ancient world.

Now and then, their dream bodies passed through utter darkness. There were bursts of flame and the chattering, it seemed, of a million voices, but both of them knew enough not to become distracted— not to investigate, not to be touched by such dream-atmospheric conditions.

"I love you," Monarch said mentally. "I love *you*," she mentally replied. Then they both felt that sudden exhilaration, that focusing of energy, that surge of triumph as the dreamtrip zoomed them in precisely on the desired location in time and space; incredibly finding the target from an infinity of probabilities.

Now was a time of special care.

Chapter Seventeen

A Together Dream

The sense of motion ceased. Monarch and Leona
tried to hold their consciousnesses as steady as possible,
but even then there was a momentary mental blackout. It lasted barely
a second. Then there was a jumble of half-formed images as their
dreamsight began to operate.

At first Monarch just saw shapes but gradually they gained object
status, though everything was gray. All of his other dream senses
operated fully, though, so that he stood solidly enough in the corner
of "the landing room."

Beside him, Leona gasped. She saw color brilliantly. Testing, she
tried to smell the air—nothing! So she wasn't quite focused yet, she
thought. Preparing to take a few steps, she rose in the air several

tumbling feet. Monarch smiled, and she floated down, apologizing. "I'm sorry. I'm all right now. Can you tell anything?"

They stood quietly, staring. Gradually the contents of the room became clear. There were several people seated at a table. "If we're right, our aspects should be here. We'd be attracted to them," Monarch said. And as he uttered those words, his consciousness fluctuated, surged, and pulled him toward a man who was speaking. Monarch stood invisibly beside the man's chair; and as he did, that individual's mind opened up to him, almost as if it was his own. It wasn't, of course, yet the sense of familiarity and strangeness was extremely intoxicating. . . .

"Watch *yourself,*" Leona cried. "Don't double in on yourself and him that way, Monarch!"

Monarch heard and didn't hear. Why, he wondered, did this man and this room seem so familiar, so intimate? As if he'd been here (and not in dreams) before?

Before he could even begin to answer his own question, Monarch almost panicked as some assaulting audio data suddenly blotted out everything else. The thunderous, throbbing rush of sound was followed by squeaking, squealing higher frequencies that hurt Monarch's dream ears, even while the rhythm of the two kinds of sound seemed to be translated into an unwieldy anxiety. For a moment the sounds seemed everywhere. Then, suddenly, they stopped.

Dazed, Monarch opened his dream eyes again. Leona was staring at him increduously; she'd obviously heard the noises, too.

There was still some static, but gradually, as they stood invisibly in the room, Monarch and Leona identified the specific sounds of the persons speaking. The earlier barrage had propelled Monarch's consciousness away from the man who so intrigued him, and now Monarch made cautious attempts to establish some kind of rapport. "I'm Monarch," he said mentally.

"I'm Monarch," John Window said, seated in George's twentieth-century kitchen.

"Again?" George asked, grinning.

"I've *always* been Monarch," Monarch replied mentally with astonishment. And again, John Window spoke his words.

"There's some other consciousness here," Seven said.

"Will you cut that out? You're as bad as Window. It's positively spooky," George said, quickly finishing a beer. "He's a . . . split personality—"

Seven turned to Window and said, "If you're really Monarch, then you must know what the Codicils are."

Silence.

Monarch was so excited that he didn't dare speak, not even mentally. Beside him, Leona said, "One of them isn't really physical! Look, that body doesn't have a history; it's flat at this level. Be careful. The room and other people seem real, though."

Just then, the dreadful combination of sounds set up a new uproar, knocking all thoughts from Monarch's head. This time the volume was greater than before, and the sounds rattled around Monarch's dream head like sharp rocks. Then once again, unaccountably, the noises stopped.

One man was saying, "You can't hear a thing with that goddamn traffic." Monarch was able to make out the words. He grinned weakly at Leona. *Traffic!* So that's what *traffic* was. . . .

George closed the window.

Seven really wanted to get out of his body so that he could deal with this new group of events, but he didn't dare. Again he said gently, "If you're Monarch, we know the Codicils are in your world, in your probability. But in *our* probability, in your past, we haven't put them there yet. Do you understand?"

Monarch tried to concentrate on the words he heard, but the floor of his consciousness kept shifting. There was only one thing to do, he thought—if he could manage it. "Bail me out if I need it," he told Leona mentally. And in the next moment he let his consciousness lean closer and closer to Window's.

At a certain psychological level, a subjective attraction took over, and Monarch felt as if he went twirling through worlds of emotions and sensations until finally he opened his eyes—to look out upon the strange room from Window's viewpoint. Yet he was still himself, and this body's senses kept the sense data clear and untangled. "I think I understand," he said with Window's voice.

But for a moment Monarch could say nothing more as he tried to orient himself. Window's consciousness was . . . truly spacious! Monarch symbolically experienced the aspects of Window's personality as separate large rooms at whose doorways he stood, staring. The twentieth-century Window faced his own time—that was certain. But in a reflection form, Monarch saw his own personality in still another room (where his own characteristics operated as Window's unconscious? Could that be? he wondered). And between the two stood

Window's Christ. Really astonished, but understanding, Monarch through Window spoke out:

"Window *can* heal. I understand now. Before the Codicils, you didn't realize that you could heal yourselves or others without . . . medicine." Monarch was overwhelmed with compassion as Window's memory-images glowed in his own consciousness: Window as a child being punished for healing a cat, the child trying to use his abilities against the greatest constraints. . . . "Oh," Monarch cried, half with exasperation, "Window identified with Christ, because gods at least could *heal.* And Window wouldn't have to bear the guilt . . ." Monarch felt woozy. He struggled to control his own subjective stance.

"It's all right. I'm here, helping," Leona said.

"Hell, that makes sense," said George, wiping the perspiration from his face. "It makes sense, you know." And then to Seven: "But why does he have to go into one of those damn trances to find it out?"

"Be quiet, George," Seven whispered, "you'll distract him."

"*George?*" Monarch asked, incredulously. "You're George? *The* George?"

George was always embarrassed for Window when he spoke for Christ or Monarch; he couldn't look him in the face. Grinning, he said, "*The* George? Well, I'm George anyhow."

"I'm deeply honored," Monarch said.

"He *is* The George," Leona whispered mentally, "and he isn't. I can tell. Something's . . . distorted."

"And then, obviously you aren't trying to steal the Codicils," Monarch replied to George, with relief.

Seven interrupted, "We're trying to make sure that the Codicils *do* appear in your time. You must be dream travelers. I sense someone else with Monarch . . ."

But Monarch gasped. The room's walls were fading, the objects falling away into images and the images into shapes that gently disintegrated. "Leona, are you with me?" he called mentally. He felt her presence—even as his body called him back to the bedroom at the museum.

For an instant, all expression vanished from John Window's eyes as Monarch's consciousness fled from his counterpart's mind; and Window felt as if he'd suddenly wakened in a new world without knowing which world it was. But no, he thought, the world was the same. George, Seven and Diggs were still staring at him; only *he* had changed. Christ was gone!

Almost incredulous, Window rummaged through his inner awareness. The paranoid Christ was nowhere to be found. "I'm not Christ any more," he said. "He's gone for good—"

Awed, George just muttered, "Yeah," because there was no doubt about it: Before his eyes, Window was turning into . . . someone else. Or into himself. Even Seven gasped. Window's eyes seemed to go click, click, click, as if changing or reflecting several different focuses before settling on one . . . and that one focus represented Window's characteristics reshuffled, put together in a new way. Then Window's eyes were calm, resolute, sure of themselves; no longer sifting or listless or frightened.

The process hardly took a moment. When Window's eyes started their transformation, Gregory Diggs had started to say, "My God," and by the time he'd completed the two words, the process was over.

But as if in response, innumerable vital yet individually minute alterations took place in John Window's posture, manner, in his lips and nose and ears . . . as if the man called Window was suddenly put together right, and all of the tensions and struggles that divided him had been resolved. Quite simply, George, Diggs, and Seven all knew that Window was now completely sane whether or not he had been before; and that this man *was* Window, regardless of the status of Christ or Monarch.

"What's going on?" Diggs asked, staring. "What do you mean, you're not Christ any more? *Ever?* You can't heal?"

Window grinned, shaking his head from one side to the other with relief. "I know what I experienced," he said. "You'll have to fill me in on what I don't remember. But anyhow, when it was over, I knew that I've always been able to heal, and that unconsciously I formed the Christ personality to make the whole thing reasonable—as crazy as it seemed to others. But there's so much more."

Seven felt Cyprus somewhere at the outskirts of his own consciousness, and it seemed to him that there was psychological motion all about; so powerful that he wanted to join it, and leave his body . . . which he kept forgetting now and then, not that anyone noticed. He said quickly, "Tell us what happened as far as you're concerned, Window."

Window grinned again. "I'm just getting used to being . . . myself," he answered. "And what I'm going to say *does* sound crazy, I guess. But I know it isn't."

George shook his own head. He knew that whatever Window would say was true. But *how* did he know?

Window began: "I used to speak for a personality called Monarch—

127

as you know. Well, suddenly that consciousness and mine merged. I knew Monarch's life, and he knew mine. But his was a world that makes ours really look sick. I've never been so happy in my life as when I glimpsed pictures of that world through his mental images. And his world was based on completely different ideas than ours is. . . ."

While Oversoul Seven was so concerned with finding the Codicils, the words "the Codicils" kept sounding through Josephine's mind. She sensed some odd familiarity, as if she herself had run across that particular phrase in some significant way before. That is, she thought, the words meant "appendages to a will." Yet suppose in this connotation, they meant "appendixes to *the* will"—to man's will?

With no particular destination in mind, she walked up the stairs to her small study and found herself examining the piles of books stacked so neatly on the bookshelves. "The Codicils," she muttered angrily, anxiously. As if by themselves, her hands began rummaging through the books, fingering the pages. Yet she had the odd feeling that her fingers knew what they were doing, that she had in mind some particular goal beyond her conscious knowing.

There was a window above the bookcase. She glanced up at it, and as if the window were a clue, suddenly her fingers flew nervously past book after book, sorting through pages. She'd never felt such a strange pressure in her mind, in her fingers, in her entire being. Then the moment came that she would always remember. She yelled out suddenly in triumph and exaltation as she found the phrase, the particular phrase, that was so vital. It was in an old book, *Psychic Politics*, by a Jane Roberts, written many years before. There it was— the blueprint for mankind's future, the blueprint that she was now completely sure was also written in the tissues and cells of the species itself. She read quickly, triumphantly:

CODICILS

(*Alternate hypotheses as a base for private and public experience.*)

1. All of creation is sacred and alive, each part connected to each other part, and each communicating in a creative cooperative commerce in which the smallest and the largest are equally involved.

2. The physical senses present one unique version of reality, in which being is perceived in a particular dimensionalized sequence, built up through neurological patterning, and is the result of one kind of neurological focus. There are alternate neurological routes, biologically acceptable, and other sequences so far not chosen.

3. Our individual self-government and our political organizations are by-products of sequential perception, and our exterior methods of communication set up patterns that correlate with, and duplicate, our synaptic behavior. We lock ourselves into certain structures of reality in this way.

4. Our sequential prejudiced perception is inherently far more flexible than we recognize, however. There are half steps—other unperceived impulses—that leap the nerve ends, too fast and too slow for our usual focus. Recognition of these can be learned and encouraged, bringing in perceptive data that will trigger changes in usual sense response, filling out potential sense spectra with which we are normally not familiar.

5. This greater possible sense spectrum includes increased perception of inner bodily reality in terms of cellular identity and behavior; automatic conscious control of bodily processes; and increased perception of exterior conditions as the usual senses become more vigorous. (Our sight, for example, is not nearly as efficient as it could be. Nuances of color, texture, and depth could be expanded and our entire visual area attain a brilliance presently considered exceptional or supernormal.)

Josephine's glance slid down the page. The Codicils were followed by comments by the author. There was a paragraph called *Comments on Codicils*. It seemed to apply to Codicil 1, and to the five Codicils in general at the same time. She read the pertinent passages quickly and impatiently.

COMMENTS ON CODICILS

Acceptance of these first codicils would expand practical knowledge of the self, break down barriers that are the result of our prejudiced perception, and restructure personal, social, and political life.

Concepts of the self and practical experience of the self must be broadened if the species is to develop its true potentials. Only an evolution of consciousness can alter the world view that appears to our official line of consciousness.

COMMENT ON CODICIL 2

This next step is as important as the birth of Christianity was in the history of mankind. It will present a new structure for civilization to follow. Christianity represented the human psyche at a certain point, forming first inner patterns for development that then became exteriorized as myth, drama, and history, with the Jewish culture of the Talmud presenting the psyche's direction. The differences between Jewish and Christian tradition represented allied but different probabilities, one splitting off from the other, but united by common roots and actualized in the world to varying degrees.

The traditional personified god concept represented the mass psyche's one-ego development; the ego ruling the self as God ruled man; man dominant over the planet and other species, as God was dominant over man—as opposed to the idea of many gods or the growth of a more multifocused self with greater nature identification.

Neurological patterning of the kind we know began with the early old-Testament Jews (known, then, as God's people), looking forward through time to a completely one-ego focused self. Before, neurological functioning was not as set; and in our world today some minority peoples and tribes still hold to those alternate neurological pulses. These will not appear to our measuring devices because we are literally blind to them.

The Jewish prophets, however, utilized these alternate focuses of perception themselves, and were relatively unprejudiced neurologically. They were therefore able to perceive alternate visions of reality. Yet their great work, while focusing the energy of an entire religion, and leading to Christianity, also resulted in limiting man's potential perceptive area in important ways.

The prophets were able to sense the potentials of the mass psyche, and their prophecies charted courses in time, projecting the Jewish religion into the future. The prophecies gave the people great strength precisely because they gave their religion a future in time, providing a thread of continuity and a certain immortality in earthly terms.

The prophecies were psychic molds to be filled out in flesh. Some were fulfilled and some were not, but the unfulfilled ones were forgotten and served their purpose by providing alternate selections and directions. The prophecies ahead of time charted out a people's probable course, foreseeing the triumphs and disasters inherent in such an adventure through time.

They provided psychic webworks, blueprints, and dramas, with living people stepping into the roles already outlined, but also improvising as they went along. These roles were valid, however, chosen in response to an inner reality that foresaw the shape that the living psyche of the people would take in time.

But as a snake throws off old skin, the psyche throws off old patterns that have become rigid, and we need a new set of psychic blueprints to further extend the species into the future, replete with great deeds, heroes, and challenges; a new creative drama projected from the psyche into the three-dimensional arena. For now we no longer view reality through original eyes, but through structures of beliefs that we have outgrown.

These structures are simply meant to frame and organize experience, but we mistake the picture for the reality that it represents. We've become neurologically frozen in that respect, forced to recognize the one sequential pattern of sense perceptions, so that we think that the one we've chosen is the only one possible.

COMMENT ON CODICIL 3

Thus far we've projected the unrecognized portions of our greater selfhood outward into God, religion, government, and exteriorized concepts. In this existence, selfhood is dependent upon sense perceptions, so that our neurological prejudice and rigid focus have limited our concepts of identity. When we do become aware of unofficial information, coming through other than recognized channels, then it seems to come from "notself," or outside.

A great deal of energy has been used to repress levels of selfhood and to project these into religious and nationalistic heroes and cultural organizations. Government and religion try to preserve the status quo, to preserve their own existences, not for political or religious reasons, but to preserve the official picture of the self around which they are formed.

But the structured reality in which that kind of a self can exist is breaking down. The official picture no longer fits or explains private experience which is growing out of it. There is a momentary rift between the inner psyche and its creations.

Besides this, the experienced self is not the same through the ages. The experienced self is a psychic creation, responsive to exterior conditions which it creates as the psyche dives into the waters of experienced earthly selfhood. Only a portion of the potential self is experienced, but different portions as intents and purposes change. It is possible, though, to actualize more of our potential.

COMMENT ON CODICILS 4 AND 5

The answers and solutions lie in using levels of consciousness now considered eccentric or secondary. This includes far greater utilization of the dream states and altered conditions thus far thought to be exceptions of consciousness. These "exceptions" represent other kinds of focuses, greatly needed to broaden our concepts of the self, and our experience of personal selfhood by increasing conceptualization, giving direct experience of alternate views, and bringing other kinds of data to bear upon the world we know. In the past, the attitudes surrounding such perceptions brought about their own difficulties. The perceptions are biologically acceptable, however, and will lead to a clearer relationship between mind and body.

131

Josephine felt like crying with joy and relief. It was as if the Codicils had always been in the back of her consciousness, about to be retrieved. And what about the book? She'd found it a year or so ago in a second-hand bookshop, and had never read it through. She had read those few pages, though, never recognizing their importance, and surely not realizing that they would one day change her life. Because her life *was* being changed—no doubt about it. She felt suddenly that she should return to George's at once.

At the same time, Josephine felt some portion of her own mind reach outward in a new and wonderful fashion. She sat down in the one armchair, almost dazed. What was happening? she wondered, because a part of her consciousness already was at George's: That portion of her mind dimly saw the kitchen, and the name LEONA started to appear in her mind in block letters and flashing lights. Now what could *that* mean?

And as Josephine wondered, Leona in her dream body in George's kitchen sensed Josephine's presence. In her dream body Leona cried out to Monarch, "I can almost sense still another person—a woman who is a counterpart of mine, a woman who possesses knowledge of the Codicils. I'm not sure what is happening, but I know the Codicils are safe. We can go home now. It's all right. The Codicils are safe."

Her consciousness fluctuated. She and Monarch joined their minds together once again. They looked once more around the ancient kitchen, knowing that the Codicils had been planted firmly back in time. The rhythms of mind-travel reasserted themselves, and they started their mental journey home, satisfied, joyful, ready for the cinquecentennial.

In her study, Josephine picked up the book again and glanced at those significant paragraphs, and as she did, they flashed into Leona's mind, and Window's and Monarch's, and into Gregory Diggs's mind and into the minds of both the Georges, and into Oversoul Seven's mind.

But it was Seven alone who saw Cyprus. She was smiling the most serene smile Oversoul Seven had ever seen. Seven was trying to keep track of everything at once. He was so excited and relieved that he could hardly speak.

At the same time Cyprus said, "Seven, look here." And Seven saw the thin hand of George the First begin scribbling on the page of the old journal. And Oversoul Seven saw George's hand begin to write down those vital words: "The Codicils."

George the First cried out: "Zounds, what luck!"

"You'll never know," Seven whispered to George mentally. "Good-bye, dear friend, at least for now." He grinned and added, "It's been a—uh—super relationship. You succeeded in your pursuits far better than you know."

And Seven knew that it was all right, that everything was all right, always *had* been all right, that it had only been their own anxieties and doubts that ever made it all seem wrong. They were all couched and safe, forever secure, forever jubilant at the heart of their own beings. There was never anything to be afraid of, if only they trusted the great sweet security that forever held the vitality of their beings, for they were all truly splendid, a part of a loving universe that cradled them forever in a safety and love literally beyond all comprehension.

Seven cried out to Cyprus, "That love is a part of all of us now. I can sense it if I don't try. Trying makes it difficult, because it's there all of the time. It's always here"—Seven smiled incredulously— "or there. Anyhow, it's everywhere, and it couches and protects the very heart of our beings. So it's all right. Everything's all right and always has been."

And Cyprus answered. "What have I been telling you?"

Seven said aloud to George and Gregory Diggs. "I have to go now, or pretty soon at least. But even if you don't see me, I'll be around, and in a way I'll be a part of each one of you."

He felt inside his consciousness, and saw Josephine driving more quickly than she should have down the dark streets toward George's house. "Do take life easier," he said gently to her. "You're accomplishing more than you realize, and as I told the others, everything really *is* all right. . . ." Seven sensed the night air and the smell of lilacs, and knew that Josephine was pulling into the back yard below. He whispered good-bye once again, and Josephine smiled to herself and drove up to George's garage. She straightened her dress as she got out of the car.

Seven felt a catch in his physical throat. He said to George, "I sort of liked this physical body. The eyes and hands and hair, the ears and all, fit me really well. But I don't really belong here this way, you know—and I think, George, you've always known that in a way. I wish you all the very best of luck, but I'm afraid you won't remember me. Not consciously. I'll be around, anyway. . . ." Seven looked at all of them and grinned the best, gayest smile he could conjure up.

133

Cyprus said gently, "It's time now, Seven. They won't remember, but they will."

"Won't remember what? asked George.

"What?" asked Gregory Diggs.

"Gee, I don't know," George replied. "I just had the feeling that something important had come and gone, yet not gone. And don't ask me what the hell I mean by that."

Tiny rays of light glittered and sparkled high in the upper corners of the room, and moved to the windowsill and outside the windowsill. They danced and gyrated in the transparent air. Then they disappeared.

"What's next?" Seven asked Cyprus.

"Who knows?" she answered.

"Do you know?"

"I know. And you know, and all of your personalities really know," Cyprus said in the sweetest, clearest mental voice imaginable.

And Seven said, "I know—or I almost know." He grinned, and waited to see what would happen next.

Don't miss these other Seth/Jane Roberts books from Prentice Hall Press. You'll find them at your local bookstore. Or use the handy order blank below for home delivery.

☐ Please send me the following titles:

ORDER #	TITLE	PRICE	QUANTITY
21945-1	Dreams, "Evolution," and Value Fulfillment, Volume I (cloth)	15.95	_____
21946-9	Dreams, "Evolution," and Value Fulfillment, Volume II (cloth)	15.95	_____
45724-2	Individual and the Nature of Mass Events	7.95	_____
61056-8	Nature of Personal Reality	10.95	_____
61045-1	Nature of the Psyche	7.95	_____
80718-0	Seth Material	8.95	_____
80722-2	Seth Speaks	8.95	_____
93877-9	"Unknown" Reality, Volume I	9.95	_____
93885-2	"Unknown" Reality, Volume II	10.95	_____
01856-4	Afterdeath Journal of an American Philosopher	7.95	_____
35749-1	God of Jane	7.95	_____
73174-5	Psychic Politics	9.95	_____
23899-8	Education of Oversoul Seven	7.95	_____
34529-8	Further Education of Oversoul Seven	7.95	_____
64744-6	Oversoul Seven and the Museum of Time	7.95	_____
18912-6	Create Your Own Reality: A Seth Workbook (Ashley)	7.95	_____
17206-4	Conversations with Seth, Volume I (Watkins)	7.95	_____
17208-0	Conversations with Seth, Volume II (Watkins)	8.95	_____

Prices subject to change without notice.

☐ PLEASE CHARGE MY ☐ MASTERCARD ☐ VISA

CREDIT CARD # _____

EXPIRATION DATE _____ SIGNATURE _____

☐ ENCLOSED IS MY CHECK OR MONEY ORDER

*PUBLISHER PAYS POSTAGE & HANDLING CHARGES FOR PREPAID & CHARGE CARD ORDERS.

☐ BILL ME

NAME _____ APT# _____

ADDRESS _____

CITY _____ STATE _____ ZIP _____

MERCHANDISE TOTAL		
ADD:	SALES TAX FOR YOUR STATE	
	*12% POSTAGE & HANDLING	
TOTAL: CHECK ENCLOSED ▶		
PLEASE ALLOW FOUR WEEKS FOR DELIVERY		

Send your oder to:

PH Mail Order Billing
Route 59 at Book Hill Drive
West Nyack, NY 10994

Phone (201) 767-5937 for any additional ordering information.